Dear Readers

Hello my loves,

Here I go again, throwing you into another one of my dark worlds. I'm starting to like the looks of this. I'm so happy to have been a part of this collection and I'm excited because this will be my first shifter ever, with much more to come.

Beau and Elora's story is only the beginning of my Empire of the Fallen Series. Hellhounds, fallen angels, demons and monsters fill these pages. And of course, love and lust. But will that be enough, to save these souls.

Please note, this is a dark romance, with dark themes that may trigger some. If you choose to delve into this world, do so with caution.

Naughty Reading,

Crimson Syn

Bane & Bound

EMPIRE OF THE FALLEN

CRIMSON SYN

Welcome...

Ten authors invite you to join us in the Twisted Legends Collection

These stories are a dark, twisted reimagining of infamous legends well-known throughout the world. Some are retellings, others are nods to those stories that have caused chills to run down your spine.
Each book may be a standalone, but they're all connected by the lure of a legend.
We invite you to venture into the unknown, and delve into the darkness with us, one book at a time.

Beau

CHAPTER ONE

You only live once...

1 922...

I stumbled out of the tavern, a pretty woman under each arm. Each of them giggled and looked up at me as if I were going to save them out of the wretchedness that the city had become. In truth, I was nobody's savior, just a lowly felon out lookin' for a break at means possible. I'd been working under an alias the last few months, transporting illegal alcohol across state lines. Prohibition was well under way, but that did not stop the greed. A noble experiment indeed, yet nothing had been resolved. Between the bootlegging and the mob-run black market, there was money to be made around these parts, and I wasn't going to pass that up.

Gin joints were my favorite pastime. Speakeasies with good Jazz, beautiful women, and excess amount of alcohol.

A perfect cocktail of degradation. This one was called the Doorway to Hell, located in a dingy cellar of a Manhattan cigar lounge. It was owned by Lucky, a bootleg gangster who had taken it upon himself to infiltrate every goddamn establishment in New York City. I laid low, outside of the gangster radar. I didn't want people to know me, I knew what that meant, and I wasn't up for no droppers on my tail. I wanted to remain in the shadows just doin' my thing and getting paid.

We managed to stumble over to my newly painted, black Dodge Roadster, bought courtesy of all the nice establishments who I supplied to, like the one I had just left. I had the car rigged for rum runs and the engine could easily outrun any copper and it did the job beautifully. Brought me to and from wherever I needed to go and never let me down.

"Take us with you, Beau." The pretty kitten on my left purred.

"Please, Beau." The one on my right batted her lashes in an attempt to convince me.

Now that I think back, I should have stayed with them. It would have saved me a whole lotta' trouble.

"Now ladies, you know I would love to make all your dreams come true, but I need to get goin', business awaits."

I gave them each a light tap on their delectable rear ends and sent them on their way. It was nearing midnight and I had to get off the road before daylight hit. I was headed on out to Atlantic City with several tanks filled with the finest rum, which I hid under the floorboards. If I was found out I'd be placed in rusty old bracelets and put in the can, and God forbid the gangs found out I was lootin' their deals, they'd lynch me.

Or worse.

The big sleep wasn't somethin' I was lookin' for.

Starting up the car, I blew a kiss to the lovely ladies and headed on out of New York City. I had one stop to make on the Atlantic City boardwalk, *The Pharmacy*. I supplied the rum and well, they would supply the more heavy-duty medications. Dope, Opium, Valium, were a prolific cocktail for disaster. A never-ending freedom that quickly became public enemy number one, and I was transporting it back into the city. Never touched the stuff, nothing but a good whiskey to soothe the pain and heartache. But that shit. The shit that fucked with your head and took away any semblance of control. I left that for the pros.

I'd seen a lot of bad shit in my forty years, but nothing like what those drugs could do to a sensible person. They left you in a bliss of nothingness, to rot in your own corpse. I only transported the goods, and with a handful of trips I could make enough to leave this cesspool of a city. As much as I considered it my home, it could take a toll on a person.

I had managed to get a nice little stash of doe set aside and planned on moving upstate. Buy myself a nice little place to call home and maybe one day find myself a pretty doll to call my own. Putting on the ritz and all that, as they now called it. Visions of grandeur, for sure. Of course, that's only if I didn't get bumped off by some dropper first. The risks of the trade. As much as I flew under the radar, I could never be too sure who was watching or who was talkin'. I had to move quickly and carefully around some crowds, especially on the boardwalk. That's where some of the most treacherous hatchet men hung out, lookin' for any reason to bump you off. One wrong look and you were a goner.

I arrived at The Pharmacy a little past three in the morning. I approached the nondescript door hidden in the alleyway around the corner, and I knocked three times. The window slot slid open, and a man peeked out.

"What's the password?"

I smirked. "Church on Sunday."

I waited a moment, and then there was the sound of a lock sliding back, and the door opened. I was greeted by a Bruno in a three-piece suit.

"Where are the goods?"

"Floorboards."

"Pull the car up."

I did as was asked and now two men came out, by the looks of it, The Pharmacy had changed its outfitting. These guys looked more like button men than pharmacists. Hitmen for the gangsters that came in and took over establishments. This was not gonna go down smoothly. I kept my head down, my face hidden beneath my bowler hat as I helped them unload the rum. When I was done, I turned to them.

"I've got a pickup."

"What's your name, friend?"

"I don't give my name out, and I sure ain't your friend." I raised my head just enough for them to see my eyes beneath the rim of the hat.

These guys were definitely not friendlies and I regretted leaving my gun in the locked case beneath the driver's side seat. There was no way I was getting at it in time. My gut told me I should leave, but I had been ordered a pickup and I wasn't leaving it without it.

"Just give me the pickup and I'll be on my way."

"See, that's not how things work around these parts anymore, kid. We heard about you bootlickers, tryin' to get in on our loot."

"Listen I'm not tryin' to get in on anything. I'm just the delivery man."

"Well delivery men get bumped."

I raised my hands, backing up slowly as they came at me. "Hey, you could keep your racket. I'm just gonna head on out, you take it up with Lucky."

"What did you say?"

"Lucky. His establishment is waiting for that pickup." I was playing with some hardcore fuel and if Lucky ever heard somebody was using his name, it would blow up in my face.

"So you work for Lucky?"

"I don't work for anyone but myself."

"You hear that, Johnny. This kid's got brass ones on him."

He pointed the barrel of his gun at me, and I froze. "You lyin' to me, kid?"

I shook my head, looking back at the car. I was two steps away; it was only a matter of taking a chance.

"I ain't got no reason to lie." Cause it was the truth. Lucky ran half the joints in the city.

"See, why don't I believe that?"

His eyes narrowed on me as smoke from his cigarette clouded them. It only took a second for him to see right through me, and the bullets began to rain down on me.

Just as I opened the car door, one hit me on the side. I scrambled to put the car in gear, and with my door still open, I took off. Bullets riddled the car, and another hit my shoulder.

I managed to get back on the expressway. I was hunched over, the adrenaline coursing through my body kept me from feeling any pain. I wasn't going to make it and

I knew it. Suddenly, a pair of headlights came out of nowhere, approaching quickly.

I revved my engine, going at least ninety miles an hour, but it was too late. They picked up pace quickly and I was suddenly being rammed from behind. This was it. This was how I was going to end. What a fucking shame. But I wasn't gonna go down that easily. These fuckers didn't know me, and I wasn't one to go down without a fight.

Taking out my gun, I swerved onto the side of the road. Wrenching open the driver's side door, I flew out, gun firing its last load. I busted their windows with bullets, seeing the driver slump over on the steering wheel as I emptied my weapon. The passenger side door flew open, and the three piece suit stepped out as I fell to my knees.

"You sonofabitch, you killed my brother!"

Rage dominated him as he pointed his pistol at me. I closed my eyes at that point, and I committed myself to my death.

May it be quick.

That was my last thought before I heard an oh too familiar pop, and the bullet hit my head, just before darkness consumed me.

Beau

CHAPTER TWO

A Deal with the Devil

I don't know how long I'd slept, or even if it was sleep that had obscured every essence of the life I had left in me. I could not recall a single detail of my death, only that I had in truth, died. I surmised I was in purgatory, wandering around this empty space.

"Hello?" I asked the emptiness, not sure what type of response I was going to receive.

"Is anybody there?"

My voice bounced off the white hallowed walls of the room I was in. There really wasn't much but a chair and a window. I wondered if this was some sort of prison. Go figure I'd die and be canned.

I held my breath, somehow knowing I was not alone.

"Who's there?"

The window looked out onto a gritty New York street.

This wasn't home, it was something else. It was like looking at it through a dirty mirror.

"Where am I?"

Patience. The word echoed in my head; the last portion being hissed in my ear.

I couldn't move, I was frozen in place. At first, I thought I was going crazy but then I realized that there was something that resided in my head. It was pacing, and each footfall sounded like loud thumbs that resounded in my ears. Being scared was an understatement. I was beyond scared.

I was terrified.

"What are you?"

I am you.

"Hell, that's a blatant lie. If you're me, why can I hear you?"

I felt whatever it was smile and it brought a shiver down my back.

There is an offer, over there, on the table.

A metal desk appeared out of nowhere and I scanned the room, my heart racing as I felt that invisible presence in there with me.

"What kind of offer?"

One that might bring back what you want most.

"And what do I want most?"

To live.

That last word was once again hissed into my ear.

"Who are you?"

A messenger.

"Of..." I hesitated, daring to utter it. "God?"

The being scoffed, and I hunched over from a sudden pain that coursed through my body.

I work for 'a' god. Just not the one that's whispered above.

"Lucifer," I uttered softly.

Among other names.

"What do you mean you work for him?"

It's a very easy transaction. I am in need of a vessel, and I chose you.

I pressed my head into the palms of my hands. "What the fuck is going on here? Chosen for what? I just want to go home. Please just send me home."

Home is non-existential. You no longer have a home.

My heart, or at least I think it was my heart, sank. I stared down at my hands, squeezing them into fists. I patted my chest, muscles still firm.

"What am I?"

That depends on you. Make the deal. It gave out an eerie, sharp hiss.

"I don't understand."

Make the deal. It uttered a threat of a growl and I shuddered again.

"Please. What deal?"

You know.

Its response was that of a rough grumble. It almost seemed annoyed by my presence. I looked up, my gaze clouding, and that's when a shadow of a dark memory appeared. One filled with pain and people screaming in agony. It was a faint echo that continued to repeat itself like a twisted nightmare.

"Make it stop."

Only you can do that.

"I wish to speak to him."

Speak. He's listening.

"What do you want from me?"

"You know what I want." This voice was present in the room, and it held a depth of malevolence that couldn't be put int words. Pure evil was too simple a term to describe the magnitude of the coldness and fear that crept through your veins at the sound of that voice. It didn't echo in my head like the other one. This one could be heard clear as day, as if though he was standing beside me.

I turned toward the window, and out front stood a man all dressed in black. Black hat, black overcoat, and as he looked up at me, his eyes were dark pools of nothingness. The look of malice on his face startled me.

"I need you as much as you need me." The man's mouth moved, yet as far away as he was, I could hear him as though he were standing right in front of me.

"I don't need you or any god."

He smirked and I shook. "Is that right? So you're telling me nothing in this world would make you give up your time at hell's gate?"

"H-hell?"

"That's where I dug you out from. You were burning just like the rest of the greedy, depraved souls who run your streets now."

When he laughed, it was a sharp wretched sound that made me recoil. A jarring cacophony of nefarious wails echoed around me once again, and I pressed the palms of my hands over my ears.

"What do you want from me!" I shouted, drowning out the hideous sounds.

"I need a vessel for my Hellhound. One strong enough to withstand the agony and suffering that comes with this demon of mine."

"And why would I ever concede to that?"

"Because if you bring me what I want, then I will give you back your free will."

I stared down at that man for a long time before I responded. "What is it you want?"

"Why, God's souls."

"What?" I asked in bewilderment.

"One million souls for yours. All you'll need to do is be my Hellhound's vessel and he'll do all the work."

I shook my head. "N-no. No." My response was adamant, but my fear was prominent.

His head hung low, and I waited to see what my fate would be. When he looked up at me, it said it all. My fate was sealed.

Another vague memory of being shot at. Bullets riddling my body, only this memory brought waves of pain with it. I wailed from the hurt the impact of the bullets caused on my flesh. Tearing it away as it pierced the tissue, shattering my bones. I barely had time to breathe when another round hit my body, this one dislocating limbs and tearing blood vessels. I felt everything as my body floated off the floor, distending and jolting as each bullet penetrated my body. I was suspended like this for what could have been hours. There was no sense of time here. I had no idea for how long this could persist, or for how long I could endure this level of pain.

It took another ten rounds before I was torn by grief, reaching up from the flames and begging to be brought down. I'd suddenly become one of the blessed souls of purgatory. Those whose soul would need to be prayed for. But I had no one to pray for me. No one left to even think of me. I had no one but myself.

"I'll do it!" I screamed. "I'll be your vessel! Just please make it stop!" I sobbed in between cries of throbbing agony.

Just as soon as it had been brought on, the memory

faded, and my body was let down onto the cool cement floor of that room. It didn't take long before I found myself screaming once again.

The demon had taken over, ripping my limbs and shifting my bones. With each crack, I lost a little bit of myself. I felt it shift and stretch my skin out. I was covered in a coat of thick black hair, its claws tearing through the flesh between my knuckles. I let out a guttural howl filled with grief and sorrow. My face was mangled, a snout clearly pronounced, and as I looked at myself in the reflection of the window, I let out a cry of anguish. The eyes staring back at me were no longer my own. The Hellhound had possessed my body, and its eyes held a frenzied gaze that glowed a deep crimson. His shiny coat of fur shimmered, causing a blurred black aura that turned into a dark shadow.

I felt myself grow dim. My mind was surrounded by a gray fog as I waited in that cloud until the demon would release me. It stretched itself and when we looked up into the reflection that man was standing next to me, A black demon with horns and red eyes who now had a hand perched on my head. The hellhound whimpered and with a deep nod, it lunged itself through the window, landing on its hind legs on the rooftop next to us. My heart hammered in my chest at a volatile speed.

You're stronger than the last one.

"What do you mean?"

At least you didn't throw up.

"You think this is amusing?"

You'll get used to it.

"I don't think anyone could ever get used to this."

One million souls, human. That was the deal.

"Just like that?"

Just. Like. That.

And with that, our first innocent soul called out. There was no going back now. The Hellhound was voracious in his hunt. Once we had the scent of our mark he would never give up until that soul was his...

Until it was ours.

The Wishmaker

CHAPTER THREE

F **ebruary, 2006...**
    Upstate New York

"Pleease!!!"

The man knelt on the soil before the crossroads. His hands bloodied; his soul broken.

"I beg of you! I will give up anything you ask of me, but please help me!"

His broken wail echoed through the stillness of the night.

This was where that stranger had told him to go. Right at this spot was where he would find what he sought after. He'd give himself up for her. He'd give anything up for her.

"Please," his cracked sobs racked his body.

Spit fell to the ground, his hands pounding against the hardened soil. "Answer meeee!!!"

A deep silence fell upon him. No signs of life anywhere. Even the crickets had gone quiet.

"Why won't you answer me?" Exhaustion took over as he fell onto the dry ground. He lay there quietly, listening to the hard pulse of his heart echoing in his ears, the stars above blinking down at him. He began to wheeze, as dust filled his lungs, and with every struggling inhale his sobs continued.

"I'll die for her. Take me! Take my soul for hers!"

A century old whisper filled the air. Its tone was hoarse and gruff, startlingly jarring as it grated along each of the man's nerve endings.

"What good is a soul of a farmer for the Fallen One?"

"I am not worthy. I know this. But all I ask is to exchange my life for hers."

Through his blurred, tear-filled eyes, he spotted what looked like a dark cloaked figure at the center of the cross-road. The sound of the corn stalks billowing in the wind hissed around him, as the faint sounds of screams danced upon the leaves. Through those screams he heard that harsh whisper once again.

"What you seek comes with a price."

"I don't have much. Just these two hard working hands." Those hands shook as he stared down at the blood that had dried on them and raised them to the apparition.

"These two hands who will work for him until the day I die."

A cold wind swirled around the man, and he shook as if ice were crawling through his veins.

"Do you believe that you are the ultimate trade off?"

"I believe I am nothing. But I have heard he has done unspeakable things for men a lot less worthy than I. Please save my wife. I beg of you. Save her."

"Why? Why should we?"

"Because she is everything. She is sweet and kind, and she will do more good than I ever will."

"Good? No man is good."

"Then take me! Use me to do his bidding."

"It is not *you* we want."

"Then who?"

The figure got closer, a dark shadow floating in the air before him. "We'll come for her when it's due time. We'll come for her and *her* alone."

At first the man did not understand, and then slowly he realized what was being asked of him.

"No," the man shook his head profusely. "Not her! Me! Take me!"

"You give orders rather easily for a man who claims to be nothing?"

The voice cackled and broke as anger swept across the man, the power slashing him across the face. The man slowly lifted his head, and he could feel a cold wetness trickling down his face. When he reached up, his own blood mixed with the one which already coated his hands.

"My daughter was never an option."

"Neither is your wife's soul." The last word was breathed out in a deep devilish tone.

"Please. My daughter has nothing to do with this."

"She has everything to do with this. She is not yet free from sin, and yet, she has already taken a life. A soul for a soul, human. That is the trade made here."

Red eyes glowed beneath a black hood as the apparition began to fade. The man grew desperate, and he reached out to grab its garbs only to scream in agony as his hand was torched. Flames lit up the flesh, only to die out a few seconds later, leaving burn marks along the tendrils of his fingers.

"You dare to call upon me because your heavenly father did not listen. He. Never. Listens!" The voice roared, causing the man to cover his ears, flinching and doubling over as the sound inflicted pain.

"*My* father has no mercy. Your first born is what he is requesting. Will you not obey?"

The man shook and the demon cackled once again, its eyes glowing as it drifted into the shadows.

"If you had another way out, then you are praying to the wrong god. This one will answer your call, but only at a price. And I assure you, that price will be paid."

"There must be something else I can give..."

A screeching laughter filled the air. "There is no bargaining with the Fallen One. You forget yourself human. You are nothing. You are less than nothing in the eyes of my dark lord."

The figure once again began to fade and the man in his anguish, crawled to it. Reaching up once again to be delivered into this evil.

"I will give you my daughter, just please, please save my wife! Please bring her back to me!"

The figure looked down on him and the evilness of the presence made him cower.

"There is no turning back."

"I...I understand." Ashamed, he bowed his head and clenched his eyes and fists shut.

"Then it is done."

Not sure what was to be expected he knelt there, waiting. Waiting on a miracle, on a flash of light, on lightning to strike, but when nothing came, he cautiously opened his eyes. The apparition had faded, and the man slowly took to his feet. He was once again alone, the whispers of screams had died away and all that was left was the rustling of the corn stalks, sounding like crashing ocean waves that filled the silence. He took off into the darkness. The soles of his calloused feet burned as he ran the three miles home. As he reached for the door, he could hear the crying of a newborn child. Slamming the door open, he rushed up the stairs and stopped short as he heard that familiar murmur of his young wife's voice.

He froze just upon that door, the faint light that drifted out from beneath it, touched his boots. Slowly, he reached for the doorknob, the door creaking as he pushed it open. There lay his wife, the sheets still filled with the same blood that filled his hands. But there she lay, cooing and murmuring at a bundle in her arms.

The midwife looked up at him, a shocked expression on her face. "I don't know what you did, Sir, but life breathed into her lungs once you left."

His young wife, his sweet Irina looked up at him. Rose in her cheeks and a deep golden gaze filled his heart.

"She's beautiful," She whispered, not having any knowledge of what he had just done for her.

For his daughter.

He slowly approached the bed, kneeling by her side. A deep regret filled his soul as he looked upon his crying infant child. He didn't know the depths of his selfishness until now and he began to weep as an unbearable grief descended upon him. The knowledge that he had just sentenced his daughter to a disgraceful fate would go with him until the day he died.

Elora

The Legend of the Black Dog

T*wenty-One Years Later...*

I could feel the pavement pounding beneath the soles of my shoes. My hands shook, my gut felt like it was squeezing the breath out of me. Every hair on my body stood on end. I stumbled, falling to a knee, and then quickly scrambled to get up, clawing at the cement as I regained my footing.

Being hunted was not in my plans. At twenty-one, I should have been happily planning my prom and making out with my boyfriend. Instead, I was running away from, yet another demon sent from hell to capture my soul.

My poor tired soul. If my father had only known what damage he'd done on that dark fateful night. He damned me into a life of fear and terrors no human should ever succumb to.

I'd been hunted since I turned eighteen. Promised to whom they called the Dark Prince. He stalked me in my nightmares, made dark seductive promises to keep me safe, and then he'd send his dogs to fetch me.

Demons.

They came for me in the dark and traveled in the shadows. Spectral harbingers of imminent death, they came in all shapes in sizes. Some appeared in the form of the ones I loved, to lure me into that infernal region that awaited me upon my deliverance. Some came as serpents, hissing its doubts into your ear. If you were weak enough, you'd falter, and that's when it would inject its poison in you. And with thoughts of suicide and death. Conniving devil would have you take your own life.

But the worst were the hounds of hell. Hellhounds were called The Bearers of Death, supposedly created by ancient demons to serve as an omen of death. According to legend, three sightings was all it took for the curse to take effect and kill the victim.

I fought them as best I knew how. My mother guarded me with her protection spells, but she was long gone, and I was left to my own defenses.

There were three rules one should follow when destroying a hellhound.

Rule number one: Never look into its eyes.

Recognizing it would only increase the effects of the curse, decreasing the time it would take for the hellhound to finally reach your soul.

Rule number two: Stay out of the shadows.

That's one rule I didn't abide by. I lived in the shadows. It was the only way I could hide from them. By using their strength against them and turning it into a weakness.

Rule number three: Never leave home without your

iron weapon. My weapon of choice, an iron blade, soaked in hell fire. My mother had acquired it from a lost traveler. He'd been to Ashgabat in Turkmenistan where he had been blessed and taken to what they called Hell's Gate. The way the fire burned there...it was clear it wasn't of this world.

The weapon had become instrumental in my training, and I was taught from a young age, to protect myself. I had become an expert huntsman, killing them by the second sighting. They never expected it. It was a clean killing. Not at all like the ones they offered me. At the claws of a hellhound, you could expect your body to be torn to shreds before they got to your soul. But they never got that far.

My mother had given her life to protect my soul and the one thing she asked of me was to stay alive. But the living walked among sin. It called them at every corner. Pulled them into its allure and as soon as it got a hold of them it wouldn't let them go, ensuring a death that would be damned.

I gripped the amulet my mother had left me. It was a replica of an ancient amulet worn by the Greek. Engraved on black onyx was the figure of a warrior, encircled with a halo and thrusting a spear. On the top arch of the frame were the words, "The One God Who Conquers Evil." On the other side of the amulet was a picture of an eye pierced by arrows and a devil's fork. It served as protection against anyone who would give you "the evil eye." The onyx had small diamonds encrusted in the stone that had a power to glow a deep crimson, warning me of the dangers that lay ahead.

I gripped the blade, sliding it out of the leather sheath that lay at my hip, running into the darkest alley I could find and waited. My entire body was telling me to run, but I drew strength not from cowardice but from the promise I had made.

Promise me you'll live, my sweet girl.

That promise meant everything to me. It was a debt I owed, that I would do anything to pay back.

Brushing the sad thoughts away, I focused on what lay ahead. It was brief, but I felt its coarse fur brush up against my side. I held my breath, keeping my heart rate at bay. A trick I'd learned on my own. The hellhound not only had super strength, but it could sense your fear. If I calmed my heart rate, they'd sense no fear, and they'd turn away, giving me just enough time to wield my blade.

I heard it shift, sniffing the air, searching for me. I clenched my eyes shut tight, breathed out a count of five, and when I opened them, I screamed. The creature snarled in my face, reaching out with a swipe of its claws that tore through the skin of my arm.

I stumbled back, falling into the trash bin behind me. I struggled to get up as the heels of my boots slid out from under me. The creature was crouched above me, it's snout in my face, a low menacing rumble protruded from its snout.

I didn't think, I just reacted. One moment it was about to tear my face off, the next it had collapsed over me. It's heavyweight making it hard for me to breathe.

I grunted, shoving it off me. Its black blood had seeped through my jeans and leather jacket.

"Asshole," I seethed, gripping my blade, and sliding it out of the side of its head.

"I hope you rot in hell."

I swiped the blood off on my already damaged jeans and slid the blade back into its casing. It would only be a matter of days when another would come knocking. I needed to rest up and see what I could do to shield myself and bide me some time.

My parents had grown up in a small town upstate. My father ran a stable, training horses. I loved my father, but he always tended to stay away from me, almost fearing me. It wasn't until the night terrors started that my father finally told my mother those secrets he kept buried deep.

My mother came from a Christian home. Her parents had instilled every type of religious sermon you could find, but my mother would have none of it. She believed in something more powerful, and she felt it in her bones.

When she found out about the deal my father had made, she'd cursed him. I don't believe she did it intentionally, but her rage and grief were more powerful than any religion. I'll never forget my father's sad eyes as my mother gathered up our things, grabbed my hand, and walked out.

My father had died a week later from a heart attack. Although if you ask the townspeople, David Wolfsbane had died of a broken heart.

My mother had grieved his death with as much sorrow as a woman in love could muster. Because as much as she hated him, she never stopped loving him. But I was more important for her, and she'd moved us to the city hoping it would be easier to hide among the throngs of people. Unfortunately, she quickly found out that Lucifer's favorite pastime was hunting down his souls and I had become his favorite.

I sauntered into my apartment above the bookstore my mother owned. We sold metaphysical and spiritual books, tarot, candles, herbs, and anything Wiccan. My mother was a powerful witch, but it never transcended. I wasn't a Wiccan, nor did I have any of her power. I believed in her and what she believed in, that was enough to keep me strong spiritually.

I guess if you meet the devil and you've seen his many faces, there is absolutely no way on earth, you could not believe in a god. As distant and unfathomable that idea seemed to some.

I gathered what I needed and ran up to my apartment, sealing myself in my bedroom. I poured a circle of salt around the frame of my bed, slid my blade beneath my pillow, and held on tight to my amulet.

I would never find peace in sleep no matter how many creeds I prayed or however many times I asked the Lord my soul to take. I learned quickly that my soul was no longer mine to give.

I stared up at the ceiling, hoping this dream wouldn't end as so many others had. Drenched in the blood of those I loved. He delighted in torturing me. I could almost hear that evil chuckle when I awoke drenched in sweat and my heart jeering in my chest.

You could only watch your mother die so many times before it starts to fuck with your head. As I closed my eyes I hoped for a different dream. One I would actually live through.

One, where for once, I'd win.

Beau

Collector of Souls

I watched her running down the street barefoot. The monster was after her, laughing at her from a few feet behind. It enjoyed terrorizing her.

I couldn't feel my hound. He was nowhere to be found. But I did feel her. Her ankle had twisted along the way, and she had blisters on her feet. I felt her pain embedded in the tips of my fingers.

Her chest had tightened, her lungs burning as they fought to breathe in the smoke that now filled the air. It burned in my lungs, just as it did in hers.

I watched as the monster cornered her. The fear that shone in her eyes was mesmerizing. The monster leaned into her, and she shielded her pretty face from me.

I seethed, angry that she would want to hide from me. I reached down, prying her hands from her face, forcing her to look at me.

It took me only a second to realize that it was me she was running from. *I* was her monster.

I stumbled back in stunned silence. I was her monster but as I looked down at my hands, they were my hands, not the hound's.

I looked down into a puddle of water, my reflection looking back at me. I looked the same as I had when I died, except for the beard that now covered my jaw, it was black as coal, and my eyes...My eyes were the color of black ink.

She screamed as I looked down at her and as I reached for her, she scratched at my arms, slithering away into the night.

I stared down at my reflection once again, this time my eyes glowed a deep red, the shade a vivid cerise. I shuddered, fearing myself for once.

I'd collected thousands of Souls. They all ran, they all screamed, but I wasn't the one hunting them. I wasn't the one who preyed on them. It had always been the hound.

So why me?

Why now?

I could smell her, and the more she screamed, the more of a thrill ran down my spine. On instinct, I began to hunt her. But it wasn't in the hound's need to tear her to pieces. This need was very different. This need was feral in its calling.

She ran down those empty city blocks, with only the streetlights guiding her path. A path that would lead her right to where I wanted her.

I followed close behind, her sweet scent of citruses lured me in. She stumbled in through the iron fence that led into the cemetery grounds. I continued in my incessant pursuit of her. This unnerving feeling came over me, as if I knew who she was. As if I'd known her my whole life.

As she fell to her knees, I got closer and closer still. She was dragging herself through the grass, her fingers digging into the dirt as she continued in her attempt to flee from me. She ended at my feet. Clawing at my legs.

"Please. Please, not yet. Don't take me yet."

I reached down, sliding the back of my hand along her soft cheek. She was breathtaking. Dark raven hair fell around her shoulders, brown eyes the color of buttered chocolate, and her mouth were two perfectly bowed lips transformed into a pink heart shaped temptation. Large teardrops fell from those wide innocent eyes and onto my fingers. As she gripped my hand I recoiled from her touch. The sigil that had been infused into my chest was now glowing a bright fire orange and I winced, grabbing at it as I tried to catch my breath.

I knelt before her, and through her eyes I saw myself. A monster defeated.

Her monster.

I tried to shake her emotions off me, but I couldn't. I felt her pure heart beating in tune with mine, and I could see in her large, effervescent eyes the reflection of my own which was now burning a golden amber.

"Who are you?" My voice was gravelly, and rough as I continued to fight for breath.

With each touch of her hand my body screamed in agony, yet the pain was the only emotion I had felt in a century. It was a harsh burning sensation that crawled into my loins and made me moan with pleasure. It was a masochistic sign of my weakness and I hated myself for it.

She seemed in awe of me, just as I was of her.

"What are you?" She asked, her voice was soft and sweet. If I still had my soul, she'd actually affect it.

Her lips touched mine and I took her breath into my lungs, and it was as if I were being dealt life once again.

She slowly began to fade, melding into the fog that hovered over the graves.

"No," I whispered. "No!"

"She's not yet meant for you."

I stared into the fog, where the silhouette of a man appeared. Everything in me knew who this was.

"Lucifer," I dared to utter his name.

"Is that who I look like?"

The silhouette stepped into the light, and I reared back. Its large angelic wings spread out above me. Its face, once beautiful, was now marred with scars that were in the shape of cruel mangled roots that traveled along the right side of its face and neck. Its eyes, one blue and one the color of blackened soot, were fixed on me.

"Sadly, I am not as beautiful as he is."

"What do *you* want?"

It crouched over me, and I winced as it reached out to touch my face.

"I've been beckoned."

"I didn't call for you."

"Not by you. By her." It gestured to the fog, fluttering its fingertips along it.

"I suppose you can say we're both after her soul."

At first, I thought that my ears were playing tricks on me, but the demon was dead serious.

"You're no angel."

It chuckled, its wings fading into the shadows. As he raised his head, I noticed how frail and thin it was. The fractures of its face were sharp. Its eyes sunken in. And the side of his face that was marred, continued to burn in ash, looking sickly.

"My name is Ashmedai, or as you humans best know me- Lust."

"You're a Sin."

"One of the deadliest, yes."

"What do you want from me?"

"Nothing yet. You're not ready for this trial. But you will be. We'll meet again soon."

"Wait!" I scrambled up just as he began to recede into the fog.

"What about the girl?"

The demon smirked. "Your hunger will grow. And like the good dog you are, you'll do my father's bidding. I'm just here to make sure the work gets done."

I was about to say something more when it raised its hand, signaling for my silence.

"Soon, Beau Kavanaugh. You'll understand soon."

Its voice faded, and I was torn away from the dream by the hound that inhabited my mind and body.

I jerked up from the deep slumber I'd been put into.

What was that about?

The hound snarled at me, and I could sense its distrust. Nothing new between us.

"You think I have any fucking clue. You use my body when you want, it seems to be a vessel for anything to get through. You fuckers are just having a free for all."

I couldn't wake you.

"And what? Did you fear for my life? Such a loyal pup, but no need to worry. I'm already dead, remember. There's not much else they can do to me."

I was growing frustrated with this game. Angered by the fact that I was always being watched and being used. I'd grown strong in the last sixty years. Stronger than most hell-hounds. I'd also been one of the longest vessels to have been used. Most got banished or sent back to hell. A little perk, Lucifer forgot to tell me about. It seems the vessel, my body, could still be harmed by magic or supernatural elements. Mostly those who had faith. My contract would then be unfulfilled, and the devil would win the game.

Not only that, but I'd also been given a broken hellhound. One who had caused enough trouble for this to be his last run.

Basically, if I was banished, he'd be burned to ashes.

We realized quickly we each had our own reasons to keep existing and in turn, we made a compromise. It turned out, we were more powerful as one.

Our charges had become easy prey and were no longer a challenge. At the rate I was going, a million souls would easily be repaid.

I thought back on the dream I had. The hellhound had a good point, I rarely slept. I grew weary and would rest but being tired was for the living.

What happened to you?

"I don't know."

You must know something.

It snapped and both of us grew irritated.

"You know, I used to have privacy. Stop snooping around in my head and worry about yourself."

I can feel something is wrong with you. You seem...sad.

"Vessels don't get sad."

Sorrow is for the weak minded. For the living, which you are not.

"Thank you for so kindly reminding me of that every damned second of every damned day." I snapped back.

His growl was low and although his apprehension stayed, he backed off as asked.

"Just point out who the next charge is, and let's get on with it."

Through his senses my sight heightened, and I sought the next soul. This one was a child, no more than a year old.

I hated collecting these souls for him. Souls that barely had a chance at life and were already condemned.

Let me take over.

"No. I'd rather the child not see you."

He's bound to be terrified anyway.

The babies were usually given to those demons who fed off innocence. It tore me inside knowing I couldn't save it.

I wish there was another way.

"Since when do you care?"

It's no fun without the chase.

I ignored him and did what was asked. Leaving the gurgling child at the entrance of the gate. As I turned away, his sweet noises became shrill cries. Deafening to those who were now damned.

Keep going Kavanaugh before we wind up like them.

And so, we went on. A collector of souls. A mere vessel for demons.

Elora

CHAPTER SIX

Dream a Little Dream

P *resent day...*

It was a different setting tonight. A hound howled in the distance. Fog lingered like a soft cloud over the grass. The sun was setting in the horizon, behind the house.

The house itself was a large decrepit looking structure. It seemed to lean to the left slightly. The wooden panels are just as old and worn as the dead trees whose twigs rustled in the wind.

I knew I shouldn't have entered the house, but it pulled me through. I was searching for something, for someone. My hairs in the back of my neck were raised as the hound howled once again, closer this time.

The door creaked as I pushed through. The inside of the house itself was furnished yet looked like it hadn't been lived in for quite a while. A dim lamp gave light to the living room, highlighting the dust and cobwebs that was layered thickly onto the furnishings.

A creak in the floorboards had the hair on the back of my neck standing at attention. Through my peripheral I spotted movement coming from the top of the staircase. My curiosity overshadowed my fear, and I followed it. It led me down a long corridor that led to a back staircase. I hesitated, not sure where I was headed but knowing that no matter what I did, I'd be forced to find out.

Just as I took that first step, a pair of large warm hands slid around my waist, and I was being dragged into a back room. I struggled, letting out a high-pitched scream, kicking and scratching at whatever demon had encased me in its embrace.

"Keep the fuck still, woman."

I froze at the sound of that familiar gruff voice. Slowly, I was placed back down, this time facing a window. The cemetery loomed ahead, a thick fog coming from a desolate forest, lay over it like a ghostly blanket.

"Don't. Run."

I could feel his hot breath on my neck, a heated caress that calmed me. His hands remained around me while his nose dragged along the inner curve of my neck, causing goosebumps to rise all over my body.

"I've spent my every damn second trying to catch you."

"Why? I whispered.

"I don't know." His deep hushed tone was a throaty whisper that sent shivers down my spine.

His hand widened over the expanse of my stomach while the other slid up the middle of my chest, his forearm brushing over my breast as his hand wrapped around my neck.

I shivered, gasping from the power in his touch.

"You are embedded in my dreams." He hissed into my ear.

He squeezed my neck lightly but instead of feeling terror, I felt comfort in his forced embrace.

"You don't fear me." He growled.

"No," I breathed.

"We'll have to change that."

He pressed his lips to my neck, the feel of his tongue mixed with his hot breath made my knees nearly buckle. There was an intense heat pooling in my core, and I could almost see his smile.

"Your scent drives me wild."

His teeth grazed against my neck, and he bit down on the soft flesh, a quick sharpness that protruded through the skin and produced pain. I screamed as his hold tightened around me and the echo of a snarl filled my ears.

"The taste of your blood now fills my tongue like warm copper. You're mine now, Elora."

"No!"

I lifted the knife over his head and just as I was about to slide it into his neck, my eyes flew open, and I shot up in bed. I was gripping the blade so tight, my hand ached. I let it go and it clattered onto the hardwood floor. Reaching for my phone, the screen came on telling me it was nearing four in the morning.

The devil's hour.

It's said that when you wake up at this time it's because there's a bad message attached to your dream. This is the time of night when the demons come out and confusion filled with anxiety tends to seep into those that wake. The devil's hour opposes the time of death of Jesus Christ. It's only logical the devil would invert it to use it for its own twisted means. The hours between three and four in the morning were the most burdensome for someone like me. And in the last few years, they seemed to be my favorite time of night.

The ache on the base of my neck and shoulder pulsed and I slid my fingers over it, hissing from the pain. Tearing the sheets off me, I ran to the mirror that stood in the corner of my bedroom.

I gasped at the sight of bite marks that now appeared on my flesh. I slid my fingertips over the wound, flinching from the slight sting. I was focused on the mark when my amulet began to glow. Adrenaline rushed through me as my eyes fixed on a pair of red glowing eyes that appeared in the reflection of the mirror.

My heart stopped. It was in my room. A snarl filled the air and as I turned to confront it, it dematerialized into a dark shadow that quickly vanished.

What in the hell was going on?

The dream had come and gone throughout the years. A recurrent nightmare that seemed to be more of a warning than a dream of what was to come.

I was older now and getting tired of running. Throughout the years I'd suffered through anxiety and depression, sleepless nights, and loneliness. I'd avoided every type of sin that existed. If I grew greedy, I'd humble myself, if I grew envious of another, I'd wish them well and move on.

That was my life now. Just a series of moments I'd moved on from. I'd hindered myself from any type of happiness, never truly experiencing life to the fullest. Always afraid of what might be waiting for me in that darkness that was so keen on engulfing me.

I lived through my nightmares lately. The dreams of that same man always started as a nightmare. I kept running from a monster but by the end of it, the monster disappeared and, in its place, stood *him*.

I never saw his face, I only felt him. I felt the beard on his face, his strong muscled arms, his broad shoulders, and his hot mouth that always wanted one thing. To devour me.

This dream had been different from all the others. This time he spoke to me, and whatever was happening between us was now evident in the mark he left behind.

They say people you meet in dreams are sometimes people you've met in your subconscious. You've passed them on the street, you've seen them in a crowd, they may have just bumped into you. But this man, I felt as if I knew him from long ago. When we would touch, it was as if my soul recognized him. It was a feeling beyond any you could conceive of.

I didn't believe in soulmates or twin flames, or whatever you wanted to call them. And if such a thing did exist, it wasn't meant for me. It had no business in my life. But then again, neither did these dreams, and he had been in every one of them.

It wasn't just about his touch. He made me want something I'd given up on. Something I couldn't have. He made me want that kind of love that existed only in the books I read. And that feeling tortured me every time I woke up, because it wasn't true. I knew it could never be. And it bothered me that I couldn't figure out why I was having these dreams and what he had to do with them. But each time I woke I was left with this longing and this yearning for when I would see him again.

Lust and desire were probably two of the most conniving sins. They were manipulative and filled with lies. They tore families apart, broke hearts, and if powerful enough, they could cause obsession, which could then lead to the most heinous of crimes.

I steered clear of them both. No matter what the man in my dreams induced.

A few hours later I had composed myself enough to make my way down to open the store. As I was straightening up, the lights flickered, and my hairs stood on end. The tinkling of the bells signaled the arrival of a guest. But it wasn't one I wanted anywhere near me.

"Well, aren't you a sight for sore eyes?"

I turned, to find one of Lucifer's messengers standing in the entryway. The one I hated the most. Anyone would run off screaming from the marred demon that seemed to hover over us mere humans, but he'd been a frequent customer in my life.

He reached a mangled hand out, playing with one of the candles, causing it to flicker on and off.

"I didn't invite you in."

"No, but your mother did. That's all the invitation I need."

"My mother is dead."

"And she does send her regards. Her screams of terror fill the caverns of hell, but then again, what can you expect from a cackling witch." He hissed that last word for emphasis.

"My mother was a good witch."

"Of course, she was. And I'm an angel called down from heaven."

"What are you doing here, Ashmedai?"

"I just came to check up on you. Can't an old friend pay you a visit?"

"I think you and your kind have paid several already. It's getting tiring putting you down."

"I heard. You seem to be having a field day banishing those lower demons."

He turned to me, the burnt ash on his face curling into a smirk as he realized I had drifted onto the protection engraved beneath the wooden table in the center of the room.

"Perhaps a more powerful deity will give you the challenge you're looking for."

"Why doesn't he just give up. I will never go willingly, and he's missed his chance more than once."

He tore a rosary from one of the stands and held it up, his eyes glowing with a red hue.

"Have you had any success in finding him?" He pointed to the cross in his hand and I clutched the amulet at my chest.

"I have other means. I don't need angels and fairy tales."

"Ahhh yes, a spiritualist. You all think you know better, but if my Dark Lord exists, I can assure you the opposing deity exists as well. You should have a look at that."

Ashmedai was considered one of the deadly sins. The very one who had been cowering in the dark while I dreamed. And he loved to get his kicks off with the twenty-eight-year-old virgin.

"Perhaps I'll send one of my pets to finish you off. I promise you'll enjoy my methods."

"I'll destroy every single one."

His eyes turned dark and hollow. "You can't outrun them all, Elora. Time is against you."

I squared off my shoulders, fixing my eyes on his. "I'll fight until my last breath."

His lip curled into a snarl. "Which I can assure you, it won't be long."

"Get out."

His chuckle grated on my senses. "I can't wait to see you beg, Elora. Because you will, just like your mother did. And your pleas will be drowned out by your screams."

The dim lights flickered once again, and he disappeared right before my eyes. The bells ringing signaled his departure.

I fell into a chair, clinging on to my amulet. The sins always liked to pay me a visit, but Ashmedai liked to come forth more than most. Why was it that the demons always liked to walk among the living, yet the virtues were always so hard to find when needed.

Were we that weak?

I slowly went back to my daily routine, hoping that I wasn't as weak as he'd made me seem. And hoping that if there was a God up there, he was also watching. Maybe he'd take mercy on me when no one else would.

ℬeau

CHAPTER SEVEN

A Doorway to Hell

Present Day...

Seated in the dark recesses of the familiar bar, shadowed in a cloud of smoke and hidden by dim lighting, I waited. I had one last soul to take.

One last innocent scream and I was free to roam the earth as a human. Free to take back my life, my choice. To taste sweetness again. To smell the saltiness in a cool breeze by the sea. To crave a woman again and feel her heat against the palm of my hands.

My punishment had lasted a century. A century of blandness. Of being engulfed in black and white when I had already known the color that surrounded me.

The speakeasy was slow tonight. Acheron, the club's

present owner, and fellow Hellhound, leaned against the bar.

"You moonlightin' tonight?"

"I got a new charge."

"Well ain't that a kicker. When does the chase start?"

I shrugged. "Any day now. I'll know when I see her."

The souls I collected had a gray shadow that lay around their shoulders like a heavy weight. For the most part the shadow would blur them in such an intriguing fashion that you were never quite able to see their face. It somehow made it easier to handle their screams. I didn't know what to expect with this one, since it would be my last.

"Heard you were getting out of here. You got a sweet deal there, Kavanaugh."

"Yeah. But something tells me it's not gonna come easy."

Acheron nodded. "You're preaching to the choir, man. I don't think I'll ever leave this goddamn place."

"Doesn't hurt to try." I raised my glass to him before taking the shot.

"Trying is the least of my worries. My sins run deep. I doubt I'll ever get to redeem my soul."

Acheron had run A Doorway to Hell since I could remember. He was the first familiar face I spotted after I died. Turned out, he too was held down by a contract. But unlike myself, who'd been forced to make a deal, he had willingly given himself over.

In life, he'd been a murderer, but he never really elaborated on it. He just told me that if he could have stopped it, he would have. The only thing he regrets was not doing anything about it and he relives that lack of bravery each day.

Every now and then he'd lower his tone, lean against the

bar, and whisper his wrongdoing. Almost like a mantra he didn't want to forget.

I let her die.

Those words haunted him, just like all those souls I'd taken, have haunted me.

Acheron had reached defeat, accepting to stay here for all eternity, while I couldn't wait to get the hell out.

"What in the hell is that?"

I followed Acheron's line of sight as it landed on a woman in the far back corner.

"You see it, right?"

I nodded. "I see it."

"I thought they were myths."

I glanced at Acheron who was watching the woman with a glint of awe in his eye. She was bewitching. With her bright chocolate eyes and wild dark hair. She seemed uncomfortable sitting there, fidgeting with the hem of her dress. But it wasn't her eyes or hair we were both drawn to. It was the soft golden hue that flowed around her. An aura I'd never seen before.

"What is she?"

"Powerful," he murmured.

"Is she yours?"

"Now one of mine. Mine don't shine like that."

I felt the hellhound's unease, as if he also was fighting it along with me. We both knew this was it. This was our last charge.

"She's mine," I lowered my tone and narrowed my eyes on her.

"Good luck, man. That right there isn't something I want to fuck with."

I glared at him. "You know what she is?"

He seemed to hesitate and then slowly brought his head up to watch her again, a lost look in his eyes.

"She's a cursed one. Can't you feel the power?"

I shook my head and he continued. "That glow means that the witch who protected her was powerful. I'll bet her soul is hidden. You'll never get to it."

I let out the hellhound's angry growl. I knew my eyes were glowing a bright red and I quickly shut them.

"It's fucking with your head, isn't it?"

My breaths were sharp and ragged as I fisted the edge of the bar counter. Something in me was stirring. It went beyond the hellhound. Beyond the gates of evil that chained me. This was traipsing on the edge of unfamiliar territory. My hellhound sniffed the air, electric currents seizing our control. Power of the most magnetic kind, radiated from the beauty.

I looked up into the mirror behind Acheron. Flames had ignited in my eyes, golden embers I'd never seen before. A wild, glazed over gaze encompassed their depths, and in my confusion, I turned to Acheron.

"Help me," I managed to utter before stumbling off the stool.

I grabbed at my chest where Lucifer's sigil had been carved into my flesh. It burned even more than it had that dreadful night.

Acheron managed to haul me out of the speakeasy and out the back door into the alleyway. The farther I got, the more unease I felt. Storming out of the speakeasy, I breathed in gulps of air. I fell onto a heap of snow, my hands steaming in relief.

"What in the fuck?" I cried out as I tore my shirt away from my chest. The sigil was lit a bright orange.

"Fuck," Acheron whispered in the distance.

It took me a few minutes to regain my composure and get my breathing back to a normal pace.

Unlike angels, if hellhounds or their vessels were attacked, they felt pain. Every pain imaginable. It was part of our eternal punishment. It was a pain I didn't know because I never experienced it before. And we felt it double because it was both his and mine combined.

"What the fuck was that?"

"Some sort of protection."

"Did you feel it?"

"I felt in the air, but it came at you directly."

"My eyes," I grabbed him. "Did you see my eyes?"

Acheron hesitated.

"Did you see them!" I shook him.

"I saw them."

"Have you ever seen that before?"

"Once. A long time ago."

I grabbed at his shirt, pulling myself up from the ground. "Tell me."

"I think we need to find you a place to rest."

"I think you need to tell me what you know."

He paused and then lowering his voice, he continued. "We don't talk about it."

"Why?"

"Because it's impossible. Hellhounds are meant to guard the gates of hell; not protect the very souls they hunt."

"Protect?"

Acheron ran a hand through his salt and pepper hair, his brow furrowed, his back taut with tension.

"They say hellhounds were first created by God as mankind's best friend."

"A dog?"

He nodded. "Lucifer took that and twisted it around to make a creature so terrifying, it would cause humanity to doubt."

"Isn't that what he usually does."

"This hellhound broke all the barriers. Sworn for all eternity to do the Fallen One's bidding, he went against everything we were meant for. Maybe it was a joke from God, or maybe he was just trying to get back at Lucifer, but in that, they caused a lot of suffering."

I could tell Acheron had been close to this vessel, as his thoughts became dark and his voice mournful.

"His name was Darius, and he was a powerful vessel. Much like yourself, he was able to tame his beast. Then one day something came over him. Some say it was God, others say his soul fought through, and others say it was a woman."

"What happened to him?"

"He just went mad, like a rabid dog. It's said his hellhound destroyed him, making sure he suffered the most violent of punishments."

"What happened to the woman?"

"Chained to the Dark Prince and condemned to be his servant for all eternity."

He looked up at me then, his eyes saying everything he felt. "He was a good man in his life. A devout Catholic, a Priest. Lucifer fucked with his mind at the end of his life and made sure to send his demons to do their worst. Damien was a suffered vessel."

I started to pace, feeling the restlessness in my hound. "We're not meant to feel anything but pain."

"He fell in love."

"Love is a fairy tale. A story woven to make humanity believe that good exists, even when surrounded by demons."

"But good does exist, Beau. You just got to look deeper."

45

I knew he spoke of it as a residue of something that he'd once had and lost. But I knew better.

"Wake up Acheron. We don't serve good. We take evil down where it belongs. After so long, I'd think you'd know better."

"All I know is that I've seen what that kind of power does. Don't be stupid Beau. Evil doesn't exist without corruption. And in order for that to happen, good must exist."

I swallowed hard, unable to say anything because what he meant was starting to make way too much sense.

"Am I going to turn into a rabid fucking dog?"

He shook his head. "I'm saying Damien had that same crazed look in his eye that you have in yours. Whatever she is, she holds something over you that's inexplicably powerful."

"She's just a human. What harm can a human do?"

"More than you might think, especially if their faith is strong."

"Alright, well then how do I get rid of it?"

"You don't. She's your charge."

"You literally just told me her soul was protected by some unknown witch's curse!"

He nodded. "So do what you do best and send her to the depths of hell."

My hound snarled.

That's easier said than done, he whispered.

I looked out into the night sky and cursed. I knew he'd make it difficult for me. In the end, this was all his game, and we were just his pawns.

My thoughts went back to the woman, with her fair skin and dark raven hair. But it was her eyes that seemed to burn in me. Those chocolate hues that seemed to call out to me just like they had in my dreams. Everything around me stopped as I realized something major.

This woman was the one in my dreams.

Elora

CHAPTER EIGHT

Hellhound on my Trail

My eyes were playing tricks on me, because at first, I didn't understand what it was I was seeing. It was only a glimpse, but it was long enough for me to know that I was being preyed upon again.

My entire body was on alert. Every single one of my senses was telling me to run, but instead I waited patiently for it.

I could tell it was a hellhound by its presence, but there was something else hidden. The being inside the beast seemed familiar.

I was prone to hunting demons. I could now sense their differences, some more dangerous than others, all with their own agendas. But this one didn't have an agenda. It didn't enjoy the hunt. Unease flowed through it and reverberated through me.

I'd never felt those human emotions before. The demons never emitted feelings. I could sense evil in them. I could tell how ancient they were by the electrical current in the air. Their energy felt heavier, almost burdensome. But his energy felt more like a golden aura. It didn't necessarily feel evil, but it definitely wasn't all good.

The beast also felt different. It was impatient as it stalked me. But its power hit me like a blow in the chest, taking all my breath in one swoop. I gasped, and then I broke into a run. Hiding among the throng of bodies that were heading home for the night.

The city was always bustling at this time of the evening, and it was easy to hide from sight, but not from the energy. I bumped into several people, one of them turning to yell at me as he told me to watch where I was going. New Yorkers always knew the right thing to say.

I stepped into a restaurant and made my way out toward the back. The kitchen staff barely saw me as I swept past them. They were too busy hovering over steamed pots and calling out orders. Life surrounded me in that moment, and I became aware of how it continued without me.

I ran out to the alley, the cold winter air swirled around me, making it even harder to breathe. I cautiously made my way to the other end of the street. I'd lost it for now, but who knew how long it would take for it to find me again.

I made my way around a busy intersection. Careful of every person who walked toward me. Each one a potential threat. I was on edge. Never really knowing what to expect.

I tensed as a man fixed his sights on me, glaring at me beneath the rim of an old-fashioned hat. His long black overcoat flapped around him, hinting at a gray three-piece suit. I tried to look away, but his gaze kept me frozen in place, a knowing look in his eye that indicated that he knew who I was.

I stopped short in the middle of the street and the world seemed to slow down around us. It was as if we were frozen in time. The wind picked up, whirling around us, and although I could feel its chill I was warmed by the heat of this man's energy.

He didn't say a word, simply stared at me, the intensity in his gaze was unsettling. His presence was like a magnet pulling me in, but within him there was something else. That sinister energy seemed to stir. Two separate entities in one. And they were both struggling for control.

In the blink of an eye, he was gone. I found myself once again alone among the throng of people. His energy had completely disappeared.

I took that opportunity to make it safely home. Stumbling into the store where Karma greeted me from behind the register.

"Whoa!" She closed her eyes, placing her hands up in front of her face as if guarding herself from something unseen.

She stepped out from behind the cash register and reached out for me. I fell into my friend's open arms, grateful for her kindness.

"Hush now, it's alright. You're alright." She stroked my hair as she held me in a tight embrace, guiding me over to the round table in the center of the room. She sat me down and then crouched down before me.

"What happened? Was there another one?"

"There's always another one. But this one felt different than the others."

I gave her a sad smile. Karma had been a good friend for nearly twenty years now. She'd just appeared one day looking for a job and as the years went by, she became my dearest friend.

My *only* friend.

She was more like family. Unlike myself, Karma was a

Wiccan, like my mother. She'd studied under her and learned about my secret in the process. My mother always knew she wouldn't always be with me, and she'd trained Karma as best she could. She was the complete opposite of me. While I had tuned in with the darkness, she held this bright light in her. She only dealt in white magic, a selfless kind of magic that focused on curing illnesses or injuries, interpreting dreams, appeasing spirits and dealt in prayers and incantations with blessings and charms. As opposed to the dark magic some demons liked to dwell in.

Being near her always brought me peace and a sense of safety even though I knew she had no chance in defeating my monsters. My monsters required an understanding of the darkness she knew nothing about.

Karma was beautiful, both inside and out. Unlike my dark raven locks, she had straight long fire red hair that flowed down below her waist. It encompassed her pretty features and kind smile. Soft freckles aligned her cheeks and highlighted those bright green eyes that looked back at me, hope shining in them.

Hope.

Hope didn't really exist in my life. I stopped all sense of hope after my mother was taken from me. Maybe, that was the reason I was still alive. Giving up hope made me open my eyes and see the monsters for what they were. Soul sucking demons set out to destroy humanity.

I looked down at Karma, cradling her cheek. She held a heart full of good intentions, but hell was filled with people with good intentions, and I constantly feared for her soul, always afraid one of my monsters would corrupt it and steal her beauty.

"Tell me, what can I do?"

"You and I both know; you've done all you can do. You can't hide me, babe."

"But there has to be something else. I refuse to believe that good can't defeat evil."

"This goes beyond evil. The contract my father has put on my soul is more powerful than any masking spell. It's like a radar that alerts any demon in a nearby radius that there's a bounty on my head."

"I don't believe that. If that were true, he'd send them all at once."

I shook my head and smirked. "The devil likes to play with his food. And I'm a meal he wants to savor. He enjoys torturing me and I just have to keep fighting."

"I cannot watch you suffer and do nothing about it. I'm sure there's something else, in those books your mother never let me read."

I grabbed her hand and held it tightly. "I don't want you meddling in that dark magic. You don't know what that can procure. I want you safe. I need you safe, Karma."

She lowered her head. "I wish I was as powerful as your mother."

I placed my hand on her head. "My mother was proud, and unfortunately that pride became her weakness."

I stood up and busied myself with straightening the books that were strewn on the table.

"Those dreams are back."

"Were you able to see him?"

"No. But he spoke to me this time. He did something..."

My words faltered as I hid the blush that slid inside my cheeks.

"What did he do?"

I hesitated, while I gathered the books and began to shelve them.

Karma came to my side. "Elora, what did he do?"

I brushed my hair aside. The bruise I'd received the night before was now a bluish purple.

She touched my shoulder gently. "He marked you. While you were dreaming?"

I turned to her. "I don't know how he did it. But I'm afraid, Karma. If he could do this," I pointed to the mark, "then what else is he capable of?"

"Did you fight him?"

I set the books down, looking off into the distance as my memory of the dream swept in front of my eyes.

"I wanted to. My instincts told me to. But in the end, right as I was about to push my blade into him, I was torn from the dream. As if something was forcing me to stop."

Karma's brow furrowed. "That doesn't sound good."

"No. It's probably the most frightening thing that's ever happened to me," I murmured, reveling in the feel of his strong, warm presence pressed against my back.

"How is that?"

"Because whatever havoc he was causing on my body, I didn't want it to stop."

I fixed my eyes on her. "The danger isn't in the fact that he can hurt me. It's in the fact that I wanted him to."

Karma wrapped her arms around me, and I held on to that comfort. Allowing it to ground me even though inside his words were already taking effect.

"You don't fear me."

"No.

"We'll have to change that."

And he had. I feared what he could do to me, but most of all, I feared what I would allow him to do to me.

Beau

CHAPTER NINE

A Rejected Stalker

We watched her diligently. My hound was ready to pounce on her at his first chance, but I sensed that he didn't want to hurt her. Animal instinct of another kind had kicked in and he was struggling.

"You sense her?"

She's not like the others.

"No, she's not."

I want to devour this one.

I nodded. "Me too."

But it wasn't in the way of tearing her limb from limb. This was a rawness primal instinct to fuck.

And it wasn't the only thing we yearned for.

We wanted to induce fear.

We wanted the chase.

Both of us were wracked with this need and had no idea why these feelings for the woman were so poignant. My dreams had gotten more and more frequent. For me they felt like blackouts, for him it felt like an eternity, and he'd told me time and time again that he would be unable to sense me when I was out. It was as if something else took over my body in order to fulfill whatever malevolent mission it was on.

I could feel magic around her.

"Witch?"

No. At least not any kind of witch I've ever met. But she does have protection. And it's powerful.

"How so?"

I felt him hesitate. *Something ancient. Something I don't like.*

"Have you ever felt it before?"

He quieted again but didn't answer. Instead, he responded with something worse. *I cannot see her soul.*

"What?"

Souls burn brightly within their vessels. It's why we tear them apart to get to them. But hers is gone.

"You're telling me we're hunting a soulless mark."

He shook his head. His eyes, always on her.

I'm telling you; it's been hidden.

"I knew it. I knew Lucifer would play games at the end. The appearance of Ashmedai meant they were planning something more sinister."

I know you spoke with Acheron. What has he told you?

Throughout the years, the hound and I thought as one. But deep in my mind I'd found a place to hide. A place where the hound couldn't go. And in that place, I held on to my secrets, including conversation and the memories of those dreams that haunted me.

If you do not tell me, I cannot help.

"The name of Damien was mentioned."

My hound tensed around me.

And what was said about Damien.

"Something about a woman."

Iliria. He whispered her name.

"You've heard of her?"

What else did he say?

"Nothing. Just that he had gone rogue and eventually all three, including his hound, were torn apart and destroyed."

Not all of them.

A deep wave of sadness swept through me, tightening my chest. We sat there quietly for a few seconds before his words dawned on me.

"You're the hound?"

I did not go rabid, nor did Damien go rogue.

"He's the reason why you've been sentenced."

Part of the reason, yes. The other part was the magic that protected her. It fed off all of us until it finally destroyed us.

Damien had tamed me. He'd cared for me and I for him. For centuries we worked together, a master and his hound. That is, until she came across his sights.

"Was she a mark?"

No. She was more than that. Unknowingly, she was our fated mate. Our love for her ran deep and we tried to live with it in secret but there are no secrets kept from the Fallen One.

As soon as he found out, he wanted to tear us apart. See, no one in hell deserves happiness. Least of all a priest and a hellhound.

"What happened to them?"

Rage. Rage came down and made me tear him apart. And then I turned on her. Our beautiful Iliria. And dragged her down to my true master's side. She suffers there at his feet as demon after demon come to rape her. He promised her the most violent of fates, and that's exactly what he's delivered.

Condemning me to watch as she was defiled, and her beauty was taken from me time and time again.

"So why did he release you?"

I don't know. But my dark lord is patient, and I have a feeling that we're about to find out

"Why did you allow me control?"

Because it's the only way we can live in peace, no matter how much we hate each other. We can never turn against one another.

"Why?"

Because then, it's game over, and he wins.

"Why didn't you tell me this had happened before?"

It's not something I like talking about, he snarled.

"What does this mean for us?"

That's the thing, Beau Kavanaugh. This has never happened before. This is new.

"Fantastic," I murmured beneath a frustrated exhale.

No matter what happens, if there's something you can take away from the past, is that you need to remember that we will always stay strong if we are one.

Since he'd chosen me, he'd repeated those same words. I once asked him why, and he'd said it was the only way he could protect me. Now I wondered if he did it more for himself than for me.

"Why would you think I'd trust you after what you've told me?"

Because if you don't, they'll use me against you just like they used me that day with Damien. He turned his back on me to protect her and in turn, he made us vulnerable. As one, we can do much more damage.

"I'm not looking to do damage. I'm just looking to be free."

I sensed his hesitation.

Then we need to keep you alive until your contract is fulfilled.

We continued to track the woman in silence, all along that century's old unanswered question hung over our head.

What would happen to the hellhound when its vessel actually reached its freedom?

From what Acheron had told me, it had never been accomplished. Lucifer had his ways and reasons for how he played his game. Because in the end, that's what we were to him. Amusement for the bored fallen angel. He liked to toy with our senses, with our emotions, and loved to see what made us tick and what made us go *boom*.

His motives were selfish, so the fact that I'd gotten this far, when so many others had faltered, intrigued every demon and hellhound out there.

How could a vessel win?

How could a soul be freed?

The whispers continued within the gates of the infernal regions. And the biggest question yet, waited to be answered.

Would Lucifer actually keep his promise?

We entered her bedroom in shadow form. She was standing by the mirror wearing a soft silky tank top and shorts. She was a curvy little thing that looked so delicate in the silhouette of the moonlight. Her raven hair was perched up in a bun and she was staring at a spot on her shoulder in complete awe. I felt all my senses heighten when I saw the bite mark on her soft skin. I held the hound at bay as the more I looked at her, the more her darkness intrigued me.

It is time.

"No," I uttered just as her eyes flew to mine.

We stared at each other from within the reflection. The

hound's eyes glowed a bright red as it drew back, ready to attack.

"No!"

I yelled out, forcing the shift into shadows before we vanished.

I wanted her.

"It's not time yet!"

I forced us away, forced him to take off, getting us farther away with each stride. Somehow, we both knew we needed to get as far away as possible before we did something we couldn't turn back from. But we both knew one thing. This was not a normal mark. This had trouble written all over those lush curves. And if we weren't careful, she'd be our downfall.

Elora

CHAPTER TEN

A Tempting Threat

R agged panting woke me up from my deep sleep. At first, I thought it was another dream, until my anxiety kicked in. I lifted my head, reaching out for the phone on my nightstand. Through a blurry haze, I barely made out the numbers on the dial. It was once again past three in the morning.

The panting started up again and I gasped, turning in my bed to search the room. A low growl came from the shadows and when the entity looked up at me, its eyes glowed red in the dark recesses of my bedroom. The shadow form stood up, hovering over my bed, at least six feet tall. He was larger than other black dogs with coarse black hair, and that ever present remnant of brimstone that always filled the air. Much like sulfur did around demons. This was nothing new to me. A scare tactic of the devil that was meant to frighten me, to bring down my walls.

The hounds I'd confronted before were vicious, aiming for the jugular without as much as a word. This hound was different. He'd been stalking me for days. If it wanted me dead, it would have already tried at least once to tear me apart. Instead, it just watched me.

"You don't scare me," my voice broke the silence, and his snarl brought a shiver down my spine.

You could expect anything from these beasts, but I didn't know what this one wanted or why it had been sent to watch me.

"You can let him know I'm not coming." I slid out of bed, cautious to stay within the perimeters of the protection circle.

"He can keep trying. I'm not afraid. I'm well protected."

The growl deepened and I smirked. "You can try and cross over," I stared at the Wiccan protection signs on the floor. "But I doubt you'll get very far."

"You're a slayer?" His gruff voice surprised me. The hounds never spoke to me. At most they snarled and growled. This hound was not like the rest. It was larger, older, and it seemed to hold back.

I shook my head. "Worse."

He sniffed at the air again. "You're not a witch. So, I reimpose that question. What. Are. You?"

I smiled. "Can't you tell? I'm a hunter."

"Of what?"

"Of demons."

His eyes narrowed on me, and I froze. There was a hint of interest in the depths of that fiery stare. It was true, I was merely human, but I had a rough estimate I'd killed over a dozen of these monsters, he was no different.

My mother had taught me not to show them any fear, for they lived off it. She taught me how I was supposed to expect the unexpected. And she taught me never to fear Lucifer's name. But in truth, I did fear his rage. Because I knew he was relentless in his search for me. And every time he failed; his rage would shine through in the form of another demon. This one, more powerful than the next.

A week ago, I could tell you I was finally gaining ground and getting the best of the devil. But that idea slowly diminished with the appearance of this black dog. This was a completely different tactic. This entity showed no hesitation in my presence. He also didn't know who I was, which was different to the others, who seemed to have a vengeance in their attacks.

Reaching for the blade beneath my pillow, leaping back as the shadow stepped right over the protection circle. For the first time, in a long time, I visibly began to shake in fear.

"Hunted humans don't live as long as you have."

I reached out to turn on the lamp on my nightstand, and as the light touched the shadow form, I gasped. He was no longer a hound. This was a man. He was older and strikingly handsome. His amber eyes spoke of a thousand moons. They were etheric, changing to a golden hue as he got closer. He was elegant yet rugged. He wore a three-piece tailored suit, leather gloves, a black bowler cap, and his demon smelled ancient. This one wasn't like the others who had come after me. This man controlled his beast, not the other way around.

His smile made my body react. It was a mixture of sexy and wicked, and most definitely deceitful.

"What are you?" I whispered.

"Can you not tell?" He responded in the same way I had.

"Hellhounds don't speak to their prey; they usually just snarl and try to rip me limb from limb."

A long, deep supernatural snarl came from him, and I lifted the blade in front of me. "Your head will go nicely on my wall."

My closed fist became trapped against his solid broad chest as he leaned in, his forearm pressed against the wall above my head. Giving me a sexy, confident smirk, he reached out to fidget with a strand of my hair. He sniffed the air and growled.

I could feel that energy inside him shift. It wanted to get out and it rattled its cages. Its power took my breath away. I was never able to feel the man before, but in this moment, I could feel both entities and they were both captivating.

This was new.

This was different.

"You fear me."

"I do not," I snapped.

"I can smell the fear in you. It tastes heavenly," he gave me that seductive evil smile again and my insides flipped.

He licked his lips. "It's toxic and addictive." He tilted his head as he watched me, "I can get used to that scent."

"If you're not here to hunt me down, what do you want?"

He leaned down, his nose sliding against the side of my neck, another growl emanating from his chest.

"You smell powerful," he whispered.

"I am powerful." I looked up at him, daring him to think otherwise.

Raising an eyebrow, he thought twice before gently tucking a strand of hair behind my ear.

"I feel I'm going to enjoy this last chase."

Placing both his hands on either side of my head he bent down, his face level to mine.

"Run all you want, Elora. Cause when I catch you, and I

promise I *will* catch you, you'll regret you ever ran from *him*."

"*He* can't have my soul," I seethed.

I froze as he wrapped his hand around my neck, squeezing just hard enough to let me know who held dominance in this encounter. But instead of eliciting fear, I shook for another reason. It suddenly dawned on me that I'd felt this touch before.

"Not right now, he can't. But *I* can. And I will take it."

My eyes went wide, followed by a stunned silence as his fingertips traced the edges of my collarbone, falling upon my shoulder. My skin seemed to tremble wherever he touched me. His golden eyes fell upon the bite mark on my neck, and his fingertips grazed over it lightly.

I swallowed hard, my hands wrapped tightly around my blade, as I watched him. He had a straight nose, pouty lips, and a hard chiseled jawline. His hair was slightly too long on top, falling over an eye. I had this urge to run my hands through it and know what it felt like to tug on it.

Pressing a thumb to the wound, I couldn't help but give out a sharp exhale as recognition coiled in me.

"I'll return soon, Elora. I promise." His gaze said it all and he simply winked at me, right before he began to fade. His golden eyes were the last thing I saw before he transformed into a smokey shadow and disappeared.

He was nothing like the demons I'd confronted before. The devil had shown his cards and they were not what I was used to. This dog, this hellhound, was different from the rest. He seemed older, wiser, and worst of all; I had the sense that he was bored. Not only was he extremely powerful, but he was seeking for someone to play with. I wasn't prepared for that. And I wasn't prepared for the thrill I felt when being threatened with a chase.

Beau

CHAPTER ELEVEN

**"Lust is of the Blood.
Head or heart have no business there."**

I paced on the rooftop of her apartment. She wasn't what I was expecting. It was supposed to be a quick soul to steal, but this...this was different. I may have been able to cross her protection spells, but I couldn't seem to get to her soul. It was as if it was locked up in a cage and I needed to find the key to get to it. It intrigued me. She was beyond powerful, and she didn't play in dark magic, she was on another level entirely.

I cannot see her soul. It doesn't shine like the others. There's not even a glimmer.

The hound kept repeating that in my head as if he, himself, couldn't believe it. I thought being near her would help, apparently it hadn't. It only fucked us up even more. I'd experienced all kinds of witchcraft, black and white. Every type of protection spell and although my sigil protected me from them all, they didn't protect me from the allure that was Elora Wolfsbane.

My sigil had burned at her nearness. The searing pain, a complete contrast to the gentle touch of her breath on my lips.

I growled, my hound wanting to shift from the mere thought of her. I'd always managed to keep him caged until I needed him, but he felt rabid when I got near her. He wanted to keep her for himself and that was beyond impossible. That would be blasphemous. She wasn't ours to keep.

"Calm yourself, dog. She belongs in the underworld, and we can't stop that. One more mark and we part ways. One more soul and we'll be free."

The devil was playing tricks on me. I was his best hound. Soul after soul would enter his gates, most in broken pieces, but I sensed he wanted this one whole. This one knew how to fight, and she was a tempting challenge. Not only for me but for him.

My hound stirred. *Let me out,* it screamed.

"Behave."

If you don't let me go to her, I'll tear you the fuck apart.

"What happened to working as one?"

Its growl made my body vibrate and the tension coiled around my brain, squeezing the breath out of me. He needed to shift, to stretch, to stalk his prey. Letting him out was dangerous. But through his eyes and senses I'd see things not humanly possible. And I too wanted to see her.

Closing my eyes, I braced myself for the impact. My body vibrated and arched back. The transformation was meant to hurt. It was meant to punish serving as a reminder of who my soul was chained to.

The hound was vicious as he tore through me. Pain ricocheted along my vertebrae as the bones cracked and curved, the limbs in my hands cracked and a sharp wail arose from my chest as the claws tore through my fingertips. I could see the beast as it took the leap. Sharp claws tearing at my flesh, gnarled teeth pulled back as he roared in pleasure at the taste of freedom.

I let out a broken cry, while my muscles atrophied, morphing into the hellhound. It only took a few seconds, but for me it felt like an excruciating eternity. My body curled inside of him, exhausted, and it breathed as I let the beast out to play.

He didn't think twice as he leaped down onto the scaffolds, tracking until he found her floor. His fur shuddered and only one word became prominent in my head.

Desire

My hound desired her, and the feeling was so poignant, it threw me off guard. It wasn't just Desire he felt, but longing.

I watched through his eyes as she paced her room. A worried frown now encompassing her pretty features, because she was beautiful. She was unlike anyone I'd ever seen before. I had kept us from her for days, but that yearning had finally reached its peak.

I could watch her for hours, hidden in the shadows while I memorized her every move, every smile, every crinkle in her deep brown eyes.

The hellhound in turn, felt frustrated. He'd never reacted like this before. He had no reason to. His command came from beyond and I had no control over that. But this was different. He didn't pounce, didn't scare her, he simply sat and watched. That deep longing was ever present, and I wondered what exactly was going on here.

We watched in unison as she removed her silk robe, a scent of orange blossoms floated toward the open window. It was undoubtedly her scent, and the otherwise cold-blooded hound became fervid in his need.

"Not yet." I uttered.

She's ours.

"You know she's damned. We're damned as well."

And as I spoke, I knew no words were truer. I'd been damned because for the first time, in over a hundred years, I could feel the presence of another. And her soul emanated brightness and love. Her soul managed to speak to mine which was condemned and locked away in a cage that only the devil had the key to.

Or did he?

That desire altered into an ardent need and before I knew it. I watched as she slid cream on that delicate skin, her soft flesh so perfect for biting and marking. My cock grew hard and so did the hellhound's, bringing forth an involuntary howl that tore through the wind.

He instantly hid us away in the shadows as she approached the window, her scared eyes scanning the streets and rooftops, not knowing I was only a breath away. After a moment, she walked away, sliding into her bed.

We waited, I not really knowing what the hellhound's intentions were tonight. After a long time, he made his move.

"What are you doing?"

He growled low as he entered her bedroom.

"Don't," the word sounding gnarled between its fangs.

Can you smell her?

"Yes."

Do you want her?

I didn't have to respond. He knew damn well I wanted her as he paced at her bedside, enticing me. He couldn't crossover. Not in this form, and I fought him with every fiber of my being, but he was strong and wasn't listening to reason.

The shift was forced upon me. Taking my breath away as I transformed across from her sleeping form. My body shivered as the last traces of the hound disappeared. But he was still there. Still pacing.

Do it.

"Have you gone mad," I whispered.

You know you want to.

I did want to. I wanted to taste her, to rip her clothes off and cover her in my scent. I hovered over her sleeping form. I was stark naked as I pressed a knee onto the mattress. Careful to wake her, I crawled over her. The hound had crossed over and I was keeping it at bay.

I had given into what he wanted. But I was holding back with all I had in me because what he truly wanted was to own a soul that didn't belong to us.

His anger filled the air like an electrical current and she stirred beneath me. I leaned further down, my eyes roaming over her face, seeing it up close and tracing it to memory.

More. He growled, itching to get out.

"Enough." I ordered.

She stirred, her eyes fluttering open. My body tensed, perched above hers on all four. It took a second for her to realize I was there, and when she did, a scream of terror tore from her. The fear rolled off her tongue and down to my cock.

I smirked, right before I leaned in and licked her lips. Her trembling body was pressed against mine, and her breaths hit my mouth in hot delectable wisps of air.

She stilled beneath me, her hands falling against my bare chest. I hissed from her touch, the sigil on my flesh burning bright. Her fingertips grazed it and I arched back, my hardness evident over the sheets that separated us.

"Mine," the hellhound snarled as I jerked us away, dissipating into a dark cloud that hovered just before I left.

The advantages of being a demon was that you could come and go as you please. The hound was antsy, and it shivered up my spine causing goosebumps.

"Never again," I informed him.

Let's just play with her a little.

"No."

No one needs to find out. I won't tell.

Temptation was a powerful thing to human souls and although mine had been taken from me, its remnants were still in me. Every now and then I could still feel it, frantic to get out. If only I could release it without having to take this precious soul.

Elora

CHAPTER TWELVE

The Harbinger of Death

I could hear the force of his gallop as he began his relentless pursuit of me. The rough pads of his clawed paws pounded the pavement as he chased me down the desolate city streets. His growl emanated through me as he got closer. My body shook in fear, sweat gleaming off my forehead as the hairs in the back of my neck pricked up. A clear warning sign that I was in danger.

I'm not sure when his panting became hot ragged breaths, or when his gallop became heavy footfalls. My scream got lost against the palm of a hand as it clamped over my mouth. My feet rose in the air as he lifted me, carrying me further into the shadows.

"You move and I *will* hurt you."

I whimpered against the palm of his hand; my limbs paralyzed as he pinned me up against a brick wall.

"Please," I sobbed against his hot hard mouth. My parted lips allowed for his tongue to find mine in this heated exchange of dominance.

His hands were all over me. Tearing at my clothes, yanking down the thin material of my nightgown until my breasts fell out. He groaned, right before dipping his head and covering a mound with that hot mouth of his.

I writhed against him, half struggling to get away and the other half of me wanting to press myself against his hard body.

His strong hands continued to cause havoc on my body. His rough fingertips running down my belly before slipping his long thick fingers into the waistband of my panties, finding the wetness I so fervently wanted to hide from him.

An arcane growl reverberated through my body and pulsed at my core. His voice was gruff, deep, and menacing.

"I'm going to destroy you, Elora."

A moan escaped my lips, and I cursed at myself for not having control. This wasn't real. This wasn't supposed to happen. I whimpered as he grabbed me, spinning me around until my cheek was pressed against the roughness of the brick. He bit down on my shoulder, as his fingers sunk into the depths of my core. The sounds coming from my soaking wet pussy, echoed in the silence.

Traitor.

That's what I kept telling myself as the demon behind me did what he wanted to me.

Tearing my silk nightgown up over my ass, I could feel his hot breath along the tender flesh. My body was begging him for it, spreading itself in offering.

Bitch.

I yelped, as he bit down on the wide expanse of my ass. Small bites that made my knees weak. I gripped onto the brick wall, pressing myself against it as I involuntarily arched back onto his face. His tongue delved into that forbidden crevice, and I was lost. My body had fallen into temptation, and it rocked back, sliding my pussy onto his tongue in wild abandon.

His grunts were feral, his claws scraping down the front of my thighs as he pressed his nose against me. His sharp inhale made me quiver.

I scrambled to clear my mind of the lust, and as I heard the zipper of his pants being pulled down, I panicked, shoving him back as I took off running.

I wasn't sure where I was running to, but I needed to get away from all those emotions that crashed through me, drowning me. A rough chuckle followed me. He got off on the chase, and as much as I fought it, I wanted him to catch me.

And he did, throwing me down onto the concrete, those red eyes hovering over me.

"No," I pushed at his chest, and he gripped my wrists, flinging them up over my head and pinning me to the ground.

He was so large, so powerful, and my delicate wrists felt like they would break from his force. He swept a hand down my body, causing me to whimper in need as I continued to struggle. Terror ran through me as he gave me a dirty, knowing smile. I looked down between us, his cock hard and thick, his precum oozing out obscenely. He would truly destroy me.

And just as he ran that length of his hard muscle through my wet core...just as he was about to thrust into me...I awoke.

Hot sweat permeated the sheets. I jolted off the bed, my thighs slick with my own juices. I groaned as I slid one hand through my hair, the other between my legs. I was so sensitive. I was in heat.

Ever since I'd been physically near him, my dreams had

gotten more and more intense. I'm not sure when the chase became erotic. Or when my body began to beg him for more. I lifted my nightgown and gasped at the sight of red welts on my legs. The markings of his claws as he'd curled his tongue along my clit. I clutched my nightgown to me as I leaned back against my bedroom door, my fingers playing with my clit. I was so wet. I'd never been so needy.

A moan escaped me as my knees gave out and I slid down to the floor. I spread my legs wide as I forced two fingers inside of me, all along picturing those red vibrant eyes hovering above me.

My orgasm hit swiftly, and when it was over, leaving me empty. I sat there, feeling dirty and ashamed.

Standing up, my legs wobbled, and my head spun. The wounds on my legs burned and I stammered into the shower. I felt like I'd been mowed down by a tractor trailer. The hot water soothed my aching muscles, and I lathered myself up, trying to get the stench of that aching lust off me. I didn't want it. I didn't ask for it. And I sure as hell wasn't going to allow him that pleasure. I was angry at myself for not fighting back. For allowing him to take me so easily.

It was a dream, Elora.

Fuck the dream. Fuck those nightmares. I hadn't had a night terror in years. Not since before I started to fight back. I used to get them frequently. Right before I found out my soul had been condemned. The devil liked to send his demons to play havoc on you mentally and emotionally, right before he took you. But he didn't do the dirty work. He had his demons and evil spirits who crawled at his feet, doing his dirty bidding. But never had he sent one who could physically hurt me like this.

I winced as I dried off, gently patting at the scratch marks on my legs, tears forming and blurring my vision.

"Fuck you," I uttered angrily, white knuckling the sink.

I knew he heard me because in the back of my mind I heard his evil maniacal laughter. I wouldn't let him get the best of me. That would only mean he'd won and that wasn't going to happen. Not if I could help it.

I quickly got dressed, put my hair up in a bun and went down to the store, searching among the century old books that my mother kept locked away in her office. They were my safeguard against anything that may want to sway me to commit those abominable sins that would drag me to the pits of hell.

He'd love that, wouldn't he?

To convince me to give into the yearning just so I could give him my soul willingly. I wasn't so naive. Lust was something that I could do without, but love. I paused, looking up into the emptiness of the closed space. Love was something I had yearned for since I turned sixteen. It was a sweet kiss, a long warm hug, the safety of a man's embrace. But I had to tread lightly. Because those feelings of love came with desire, envy, and greed, and I'd avoided all of them until now.

His eyes glowed a dark golden hue in my mind. They were kind and curious. His scent was on me. A woodsy earthy scent, that I kept coming across wherever I went, and I knew he was nearby. As if he were hiding in those shadows, watching me, waiting for the right time to pounce on his prey.

I wanted to ignore it all. I needed to focus on these spells to repel him. To shut him out. But as I turned the pages to those books, I knew that nothing would take away the longing that now dwelled inside of me.

Shutting the books, I grabbed my jacket and went to the

one place I knew would have the answers I was searching for.

The public library.

❀

I needed to remind myself that I was safe here. He wouldn't just take me. He was on a hunt and as his prey I had to play the part.

The heels of my boots echoed along the wide expanse of the main hall. I quickly made my way down the empty corridors and towards archives. I needed to find out more about this man.

Who had he been?

Why had he been chosen?

His New York accent had a twinge to it that melted off the tongue similar to that of a nineteen twenties gangster. He hid it well, adjusting it to mimic an earlier time period. I started there, searching the archives. I spent hours searching through old newspaper clippings, not realizing that darkness had quickly fallen.

It wasn't until five hours into my search that I flipped across a newspaper slide. The headline read:

Murder on the Atlantic City Expressway

Forty-year-old male, Beau Kavanaugh, convicted felon, and bootlegger
was announced dead this morning from a bullet to his head.
His body was stolen from the morgue early the next morning.

Police are searching for those who took his body.
Five-thousand-dollar bounty for those who procure any
information on the whereabouts of those responsible.

I stared at the image on the screen. Sure enough, it was the man who had been sent to hunt me down. He'd been handsome back then, just like he was now. A chiseled jawline, disheveled dark brown locks, a sly look in his gaze, and that dirty smirk he wore so well. He didn't have tattoos back then, unlike now. And he was clean cut, much unlike the beard he wore now. But it was his eyes I recognized. They held that same deep intensity I'd seen only a few nights before. They were different in this image. This image held a glint of life, something that was long gone. All that remained was an emptiness that ran through my bones straight to my heart.

"He was a handsome fella, wasn't he?"

I jumped at the sound of his voice in my ear. I froze, feeling him behind me as he crouched down, sliding his hands along the armrests of the chair.

"They never found the guy, I did though. Ten years later. He was begging me not to take him. I had the pleasure of ripping each one of his bones out of its sockets."

"Jesus," I let out a shocked exhale.

"Nope, I can assure you he had nothing to do with it." His eyes drew down from the image on the screen to me. "Now why'd you have to go fishing around?"

"I wanted to know your secrets," I murmured.

His fingers lingered on my collarbone, and I shivered as he brushed my hair out of the way, revealing my neck. I clung to the edge of my seat as goosebumps threatened to pervade my tender flesh.

He leaned into me, his beard caressing my shoulder. I gripped onto the arms of the chair, keeping myself from showing any sign that he affected me.

"You've been a very bad girl, Elora. What should we do about this?"

I whirled around in the seat, now facing him. "You didn't sell your soul, did you?"

"Does it matter?"

"Possibly."

"Why do you want to know?"

"Tell me how you became a hellhound."

He lowered his handsome face to mine and the color of his eyes shifted to that golden hue.

"And why would I do that?"

I took a chance with my response. Knowing full well it was nearly impossible to do. But he both entranced and excited me, and if I could get him off my scent then maybe I could beat him.

"Because then maybe I could help you find your soul."

He took a step back, the stunned look on his face was gratifying, and I watched as confusion swept in.

"You're lying."

"Why would I lie?"

"Cause you're a conniving minx who will do anything in her power to throw me off my pursuit. My soul ends right here, with you, little girl. You're my last contract."

My eyes widened; my mouth went dry. "Your last soul."

He leaned in, his eyes dark, a warm amber glow pulsed in his pupils, that devilish smirk playing on his lips.

"That's right, pretty girl, and I'm going to take my time with you. I promise, when I'm done, you'll hurt so good you'll beg for me to drag you down into those depths of hell you tend to loathe so much."

Without that said, he once again disappeared. Leaving me to my elicit fucked up thoughts, and the wet mess that now soaked through my panties.

Grabbing my purse, I cursed him and the hell he came out of.

Beau

CHAPTER THIRTEEN

"Secrets are best left between the shadows and the souls."

What fucking game did she think she was playing at. As if I'd believe a mere human could find my soul.

But what if...

"Shut up," I ordered the hound.

We'll be able to keep her.

His thoughts were beyond tempting. Too good to be true. But his need came out of a self-serving existence that would only be beneficial to his dark demon.

"Fuck off," I breathed.

She wants to help. No one has ever offered that before.

"Nor will I ever take it. Indulging in thoughts like that will make us bound to *him* forever."

As if he doesn't know already.

I ignored his obnoxious chuckle while I rode the train downtown. I'd chosen to live in New York City. It was familiar territory. The closest to home I would ever get. It also contained a thousand faces that could be forgotten in a blink of the eye, including my own.

I made my way down to *A Doorway to Hell* and took my seat in the darkness. I ordered the same thing I had ordered since I first stepped foot in here.

A Corpse Reviver.

Gin and absinthe filled my tongue and I let the liquid heat heal my emptiness. I waited for her to show up and she did, like she did every Saturday since I'd met her. She'd been meeting with a new client. A man whom I didn't recognize. They'd talk, she read his cards, and he'd leave. Then she'd sit there in her dark corner of the room, sipping on a gin and tonic while watching the crowd. I knew this because I'd come in every Saturday, waiting on her. I knew every step she took, everywhere she went.

There was a pleasure I took in letting my marks know that I could find them anywhere. That they weren't safe. That they couldn't run. But Elora, I wanted to taste that fear off her once again.

When she entered the room, she stopped fucking time. My whole purpose became her. She wore a long, flowy black skirt that fluttered open as she walked, giving me glimpses of those toned thighs. She had on a white tank top and vest that was three sizes two small and hugged her ample breasts perfectly. My cock groaned at the sight of her cleavage and the hound stirred. She smiled to herself as she watched a couple greet one another, those lips painted a perfectly blood-soaked red that made me want to force her down on her knees and make her paint my cock with them, while she begged me to take what I wanted from her.

Her eyes lingered on another couple who were getting frisky at the bar. The man's hands were caressing the woman's bare thighs, until it disappeared between her legs.

My mark shifted, crossing, and uncrossing her legs, causing the hound to growl.

She's primed. Go after her.

"Not yet" I ground out.

Taking another sip of the drink, I watched anxiously as the bar filled with the usual patrons. Pretty women nervously fidgeting on seats waiting on their dates to arrive. Businessmen boasting about the stock market and how many millions they'd made that day. Men that sulked in the shadows, seeking out who to force their perversions upon.

I memorized every nuance about her. The way she continued to fold and unfold the napkin while cleaning the drops of condensation off the table. The way she shyly glanced up at a waiter and requested a second drink. The way she untucked her hair, allowing it to cover part of her face while she continued to enjoy her time alone.

Now? My hound growled at me, and I smiled.

"Patience. I want to play."

Yessss. He hissed and I could sense the anticipation, only heightened by my own.

I made my way over to her table, stepping into her line of sight. Her eyes widened as I took the seat across from her. We stared at one another for a long while before she spoke.

"What are you doing here?"

I shrugged. "I could ask you the same thing."

"You're not welcome anywhere near me."

"Is that so?"

Leaning toward her, I lowered my tone. "No one comes to Hell's Doorway unless they are looking to sin. Is that what you're looking for, sweet Elora? For a little sin."

I dragged a hand through the slit of her skirt, wrapping it around her bare thigh as I slid it up right to where my claw marks ended. She gasped, attempting to shove my hands away to no avail.

"Don't touch me."

"That's not what you were whispering last night."

She blushed and quickly looked away.

"I enjoyed the taste of you, Elora, but my hound may need a taste too. What do you say, a quickie out back before I drag you down to your fated damnation?"

"I will never give into you freely."

"I can still hear you beg me, sweets." I squeezed her thighs and she jumped.

Pulling away, I signaled to the waiter for two more drinks.

"Don't get comfortable, I'm not staying."

Grabbing her purse, she attempted to get up, but grabbing her hand, I pulled her right back down.

"You are not going anywhere. I am not done with you yet."

She looked down at the grip I had on her wrist, and I slowly released her. We stayed quiet as our drinks were set down on the table.

"I will stay under one condition."

"And what would that be?"

"You answer all my questions."

I held her gaze and then smiled. "Since we're opening up, then I expect your honesty as well."

"A demon talking about honesty?"

She gave out a lighthearted laugh, the sound warming up my body as she threw her head back. A dream-like memory of her appeared, doing the exact same thing while I was feeding off her.

"We're nothing but not honest."

"You are all liars."

I clucked my tongue and shook my head. "We only point out your truths, and most humans don't like that."

"And use them against us."

"We only plant suggestions. You all have the choice to submit to it or not, just like you submitted to mine last night.

She looked at me angrily and when she spoke, her tone was full of sweet poison. "You took what you wanted without permission."

I smirked. "I don't need your permission, sweets. Have we not established that already?"

"So you would have raped me, taken my virginity, and that would have been a suggestion."

"Is that a question or are you trying to tempt me?"

She narrowed her eyes on me. "You know that what happened between us was not warranted."

I leaned into her. "No, it wasn't, it is simply taking what is mine."

"I am not yours."

"Your marks..." I gestured at her neck and thighs. "Say otherwise."

"Why do you continue to stalk me?"

"Why not? No one here? is going to stop me." I sipped on the absinthe.

"Why not just attack me? I promise I'll make your death swift."

I chuckled, the acid in her words exciting me. "We're both here, Elora. Me and my hound. Why not take a stab at me? See what happens."

She searched the room and took a gulp of her drink before fixing her eyes on me. "I'm not going to play into your twisted mind tricks. We both know how this game is played. You attack me, I protect myself, and on and on the cycle goes..."

"Until I stop it."

We looked at each other and she frowned. "Ashdemai said that…"

"Ashdemai has no business here!" I slammed my hand on the table, cutting her off.

"You know him?"

"I know him, yes. And he is not someone you want to be quoting. Talk about manipulators, he is top notch in his mind tricks."

"And you're not?"

I leaned forward, our faces only inches from each other. "You create dreams to lure me through them. I've never seen a hellhound do that."

"You think that's me. I don't create dreams, Elora. I only chase you in them."

"So then how…"

"I don't know," I pulled away from her and sat back in my chair.

"I have no idea what is happening or why."

"I believe it's Lucifer who is using us…"

"As pawns," I finished her sentence. "Yes, I believe that too."

"But why?"

"Maybe he knows something we don't."

"You said I was your last charge. You're powerful, I'll admit that. But why haven't you taken me yet?"

I looked at her, not wanting to divulge all my secrets. Not wanting to let her know that we couldn't find her soul and had absolutely no idea where the fuck she was hiding it.

"I'm biding my time."

"For what!" She hissed, leaning toward me.

I leaned forward, right until our faces met and our breaths danced along our lips.

"For when I savor every inch of you."

Our lips touched as I spoke the words, and the electrical current that swirled around us, intensified.

"I won't let you catch me again," she breathed.

I grazed my lips against hers as they parted. "We'll see about that."

"Why?"

"Because for the first time in over a century, I can feel something."

"For me?"

I closed my eyes, allowing my hellhound's senses to heighten, and I inhaled the scent of citruses mixed with that faint essence that was solely hers. It took me a few seconds and I was finally able to tear myself away from her.

Standing up, I looked down into those pretty eyes. "Don't bother paying. Your money's no good here."

"I'm not done with my questions."

I bent down over her, once again bringing my face level with hers, our lips whispering against one another.

"Believe me, I'm not done with you either. And by that God that humanity is so fond of...I don't think I'll ever be done with you."

I turned and signaled to Acheron to put the drinks on my endless tab.

Is it my turn now?

"Almost."

The hound shifted and I let my calm come over us. We stretched out and merged into the shadows. Waiting for our prey.

Beau

Creatures Crawl in the Night

As the night came to an end, I snuck out of the bar and waited in the gathering darkness which had become my friend so long ago.

I didn't know what I had come to do. I wanted to scare her, but that thrill was overcome by a strong desire to tame her wildness. To hear her moan my name as I knotted inside of her, the hellhound shifted slightly as we both took her at once.

What the hell was I thinking?

The demon was playing havoc with my emotions and yet, her nearness made me want to feel something, anything, once again.

She turned left then right, clearing her surroundings before choosing her path home. This time she'd chosen my favorite path, right alongside the cemetery.

What are we going to do to her?

The hellhound salivated as I kept to the shadows a few

feet away. I followed her scent much like a dog follows its owner. Now that was an odd concept. One, I didn't care for.

As she rounded the corner, I paused and watched as she cut through an opening in the barb- wire gate. She entered the confines of the dead and my curiosity piqued.

I followed her in, careful to disturb the dead. When they noticed you were around, those that were in purgatory could always be heard screaming for forgiveness.

I kept as quiet and as undetected as possible. She walked up a hill and then paused at the top. My senses heightened and the hound listened as she greeted her mother.

"I know you're watching, Mama. And I need your help. I don't know where this man came from, but he holds a demon that weighs him down. I'm the last soul he needs to complete his contract, which means he has everything to gain from my fallout. I ask for your divine protection tonight."

Placing two white candles side by side, she began to pray. White was the sign of purity, and the prayer was a Veneration Prayer of protection.

I am root of your root,
Soil of your soil,
Bones of your bones,
Blood of your blood.

She repeated the words, digging her hands into the soil and digging a hole. She placed a small bag in the center. My hound grimaced at the strong stench of the bird's bones.

And then she took a blade and raised it to the moon that shone brightly down on her, she pressed that sharp edge to her flesh. The scent of copper filled the air, telling me she'd drawn blood.

She continued to say her spell as drops of crimson fell onto the bones.

I ask for protection among the wicked.
I cast this spell into the night,
To bind my enemies and limit their fight.
I hereby call all my power back to me,
Of all evil influences may I be free.
As I will,
So mote it be.

I could feel her magic swirling around me. My hound paced in its locked cage, anxious and agitated. While he was whining, I was curious to see what would happen when she realized her power didn't work on me.

She filled the hole with dirt. Blessed her mother and went on her way.

She's powerful. My hound snarled.

"Only if you believe in all that sorcery bullshit. Stay calm. It will pass."

My skin prickled, a painful reminder that I was merely a vessel. The sigil of Satan, burned onto my flesh by the Dark Prince himself. I was a lost soul, one who was dragged from one hell into another. A rarity among his throng. People forget, Lucifer was once an angel. His sigil was a brand. A sealing of a contract. It held supernatural powers and protections that the most blessed of spells could not surpass.

My hound, on the other hand, was not branded. He was an entity who was meant to control the vessel. But my hound had been weak from the start. A recluse himself, we were thrown together with the expectation that we would both fail. At first it was a struggle, I was bound by him, forced to shift and beg. It wasn't until our first encounter with a witch that I felt my power. Between the two of us, we were able to survive and trap her soul. Ever since then, we have had a mutual understanding. And neither one controlled the other. We had become one. Even though, every now and then, I found myself lost in a power struggle between bad and worst. For the most part, I'd win. But lately...

When it came to Elora, I wasn't sure I could control him. No matter what, I had the advantage. I was the vessel and he needed me more than I needed him.

I fell in stride with her. Snow had begun to fall, its flurries shining brightly under the dim yellow streetlights. She crossed the street quickly, her boots clicking on the wet pavement. I spotted her only a few feet away and I sensed she knew she was being tracked. Looking over her shoulder, she looked startled by my dark silhouette and took off running.

My hound leapt with joy as I took off after her. Long, even strides as my feet hit the pavement. Her scent mixed with her fear, lured us in.

Let me shift, he snarled.

"Not yet" I growled back.

Unknowingly, I wanted her for myself. I know that now, but at that moment, I was blinded by a relentless need to hunt her down on my own, without the hellhound. No one could have her but me.

She took a right, toward a back alley and I slowed. I could hear her ragged breaths on the other side of the brick wall, and I placed my hand to it. Caressing it as if I were caressing her.

I could sense her tension, smell her fright, and it was an arousal I'd never experienced before. I stepped around the wall just as she swung, but my hound was prepared. She cried out as we yanked the wooden panel out of her hand.

Oh, how she liked to fight. I loved every unexpected move. We stalked her until she fell back against a doorway. Quickly turning to it, she slammed her fists against it, attempting to open it. I stood back, amused. My chuckle made her freeze.

I stepped into the doorway, trapping her there with my body. I wrapped my hands around her fists, forcing them flat against the metal. I dragged my nose into her hair, taking a long inhale.

"You honestly think you can run from me?"

She shivered as I trailed my hand down her side, taking my time as I traced the swell of her hip.

"You can't take me. Is this what your sick perverted mind wanted?"

"Not quite," I nipped at her ear, feeling her body tremble.

"You already know I won't give you what you want."

"Hmmm, is that so?" I hummed. My hand fisted her skirt right at the slit.

"Don't," she struggled against me. My hellhound snarled but remained quiet, enjoying the little shudders of unease she gave off.

She wasn't terrified.

Not yet.

I slid my hand down to the sweet crevice between her legs and grunted. "Now a good girl doesn't behave this way."

"Please," she begged.

I smiled to myself as I slid my fingers down into her soaked panties.

"Please, what?"

She whimpered as my fingers delved through her wetness.

"Please, forgive me?"

She whimpered again, this time biting her lip as I slid over her clit.

"Please, fuck me?

I dipped my fingers inside of her and she arched back, her forehead pressed to the metal door.

"Please, take my soul?"

I yanked her head back against my shoulder, so she could watch as I licked her juices off my fingers. The taste of her caused havoc in my hound as he begged to be let out.

"Down, boy," I whispered as my lips hovered over hers.

The touch emblazoned the sigil on my flesh, lighting it on fire. It hurt, but not having her near hurt more. I licked my lips, and her eyes went wide.

A knowing smile slid across them. "Pure as a virgin. No wonder Lucifer is so adamant to have you."

"Fuck you," she seethed.

"Now that's a tempting invitation."

"I will never submit to you."

"Shhhh," I pressed my lips to hers and she quieted instantly.

"Soon, Elora. Soon I'll quench that sweet ache we both yearn for."

I left her there, running away as fast as I could, allowing

the hound to stretch free. He was angry, confused and aroused. Much like his vessel. The taste of her virginity was our undoing. And as he leapt through the darkness, we both knew it wouldn't be long until we'd both condemn ourselves to her mercy.

Elora

CHAPTER FIFTEEN

The Gilded Bird Cage

"So he's hot?"

I stared at Karma, who was watching me pace, a bemused look in her eye.

"Is this funny to you?"

She smiled. "Watching you squirm is slightly amusing. You have a crush, it's cute. I've never seen you so flushed."

"I didn't come to you for this."

I grabbed my purse and as I ran past her, she grabbed at it and pulled me down into a seat.

"Oh, stop it. I'm just teasing you. I've never seen you react this way to a...*dog*...before."

"Ugh!" I slammed my head down on the table.

She patted my head before continuing to file her nails. "Go figure you'd be the one to lose her virginity to a demon."

"He's not a demon, he's a dog."

"A hellhound. One who guards the gates of the Underworld. A fucking devil's soldier has the hots for you."

She smirked as I threw incense cones at her. "Hey!"

"What do I do, Karma? I have nowhere to go here."

She stopped her filing and focused on me. "You need to stay strong, Elora. You need to remember that your mind is more powerful than your body. Your body will betray you."

"Great words of wisdom. So tell me all-wise-one. How do I prevent my body from betraying me?"

Twirling around, she grabbed one of her spell books from on top of the bookshelf. Flipping the pages, she murmured to herself, and then suddenly stopped, her finger hovering over a page.

"I'm afraid there's only one loophole to counter lust."

"What's that?"

She looked up at me, a gentle cadence in her voice. "Love."

"Right. So basically, I'm fucked."

She shrugged, snapping the book shut. "In more ways than one."

She sat down across from me and grabbed my hand. "Don't let him get to you."

"You don't understand. I've run for years. I'm tired. This is the first time one of them has actually gotten this far."

"Sometimes spells and amulets aren't enough. Maybe search for a different route."

"He's got his own protection. I could feel his power when he's near." I lowered my voice as I leaned forward. "I can feel the Hellhound."

"What do you mean?"

"It stirs inside him, as if trying to get out. He's strong and he keeps it at bay. But I could feel it too. I could feel it clawing its way out, and it seems confused and disoriented."

Karma pulled back from me. Her eyes held a hint of bewilderment and awe.

"Why are you looking at me that way?"

"Because I think your power isn't wielded in books and spells. You said your mother cast a protection spell on your soul."

"Yes."

"How exactly?"

"I don't exactly know how she did it. But she called upon the angels."

Karma stared down at me. "Angels are warriors. They're soldiers of God. They're tamers of beasts."

"What?"

She rummaged through the bookshelves, taking out several books until she finally settled on one. Her brow furrowed as the book of black magic sat before us.

"What is that?"

"Your mother was a smart woman. She knew what you were up against."

"She did, and she taught me how to use white magic to protect myself."

Karma gave me a sad smile, reaching out to touch my cheek. "Sweet, naive girl. There's only one way to fight fire with fire."

I felt that tingling in the air as it filled with an energy I hadn't felt before. It was heavier, more intense. She closed her eyes and took a deep breath before she dove in, searching in its recesses for an answer. A dried flower fluttered out, landing in my hand.

It was an Iris, my mother's favorite flower. I looked up at Karma who stood frozen on that page. Standing, I leaned over her shoulder to read.

Cruentas

It was Latin meaning bloodthirsty. It was a spell. A protection spell but unlike any I surmised. This spell called for a hellhound to protect a soul.

"She couldn't have..."

I looked at Karma who in turn, stared at me. "When you can't beat the devil, join him."

Her words made me shudder. "That makes no sense. I've had dozens of Hellhounds come after me. I've fought them all. Each one more vicious than the next. What makes this one special?"

"You said it yourself. This one has everything to gain from destroying you."

"This makes no sense."

"If I told you God works in mysterious ways, would that make a difference?"

I gave her a disapproving side glance. "That doesn't help."

"Your mother didn't protect your soul. She hid it, for as long as she could. Maybe this man, hellhound, was meant to find it."

"I don't know what to do with that information."

"I've seen you fight for your life, Elora. God's protection runs out eventually. You're tired. You're worn out. You're exactly where you need to be for those demons of self-doubt to come knocking. You can't fight this alone anymore. If what the book says is true, then you have a lot more protecting you then simple sage and black obsidian. You have a demon all your own, who may not know it yet, but he may just be your savior."

She patted my hand and stood up. "I'll leave you to it."

She grabbed the bag of incense cones and a bag of dried herbs. She shook the bag in the air. "For my current headache."

I rolled my eyes as she waved and disappeared. The tinkling of bells, hanging by the door, announced her departure.

I stared down at that book. One, which I had been forbidden to read. As I pulled it toward me only one phrase popped into my head. A quote from a movie I loved. Unease rolled over me as I opened the book.

No harm ever came from reading a book.

Beau

CHAPTER SIXTEEN

He who saves a soul, saves his own.

The screams filled the silence as I trudged along the damp grass. My boots crunched on the broken twigs. The tree branches swayed menacingly above me.

They say the cemetery was a place of peace, but for a soulless man and his demons, it was a place of torment. A place where those tortured souls could reach up and pull you down with them.

There were times when I felt bad for them. Some I'd taken were criminals and violent murderers. Others were that of sinners who'd given in to greed or sloth. Some made their own deals. And then there were those who were promised. Innocent souls who had no knowledge that their loved ones had sold them off for a dollar or a title. Some for fame and some for glory. But almost always, it was due to their own selfish needs. If they only knew that they were merely prolonging death and the flames of hell that awaited them.

I felt bad for those souls. They didn't deserve to be hauled down into that abyss. And I cursed their god every day for allowing that to happen. For allowing demons like the one that dwelled in me, to come and destroy a life. Souls were kept in an area where Lucifer would judge them. For the most part they'd continuously suffer the pain of those they hurt. But for those innocent souls. They would suffer fear. A fear so deep it would send them into madness.

The blessed souls of purgatory, they call them. They'd reach out from the flames to beg for forgiveness.

Their sorrow was overwhelming.

Their fear was unimaginable.

As I walked among them, I welcomed the screams tonight. The dreams had gotten worse. Her screams of pain as the flames engulfed her. Her hands reached out for me, tugging her down with me. My soul seemed chained to hers for some reason or another.

I was confused and although I always felt bound by the contract, it now felt suffocating. Even my hellhound wasn't satisfied with a shift. I could feel his angst as he curled along my spine. He was quiet tonight. Also contemplating what these feelings were.

I found myself in front of her mother's grave. And I bent down on one knee, touching the earth where she'd been a few nights before. The energy was thick and there was a scent of irises that permeated the air. It was a familiar scent. One that stayed with me right before I died. It floated in the air before me, offering me comfort where I had none.

I could have sworn I didn't owe anyone anything in this life. I'd spent years pondering that thought but I could never put my finger on why I had that sentiment. It was all pervading. Like a heavy weight on my chest, I couldn't get rid of.

I never spoke to God. But if one existed, I wondered if this was his plan. If he understood why I felt this sense of protection over this woman, I barely knew. Because I sure as hell couldn't comprehend it.

I left the tomb and walked further into the cemetery, thinking I was alone.

"She arouses you."

I froze, as the voice came out of nowhere. My hound stayed calm yet vigilant.

"She likes you."

The voice mocked, chuckling maliciously. I hated that sound and he knew it.

"She must have tasted heaven sent."

"Not like it matters." I muttered, searching the cemetery around me.

"Oh but it does. More than you know. Tell me, Beau, did you like that she was a virgin?"

A silhouette of a man appeared in the distance. Lucifer appeared in many forms, some seen and some unseen. In this case, he shielded his face as he lounged on a tombstone.

"You knew this would happen, didn't you?"

"I suspected it."

"Why?"

"Because I want to see her fail."

"You promised this was my last one."

His laughter once again was dark and filled with an ominous threat.

"You can't be so naive to think I'd make it easy for you."

"She's stronger than the others."

"Yes, she is." I could sense the evil joy coming from him.

"I know you sent Ashmedai to us."

"He's not easy to resist, is he?"

"She won't give into whatever game you're playing."

"She won't, but you will. And ohhh, how I'll enjoy watching you both fall."

"Why?"

"Isn't that the infamous question? Why am I alive? Why is life unfair? Why did you do this to me? Ultimately, because I fucking don't give a shit about either of you. It's just fun to watch."

"You know something, don't you?"

"Now that's the type of questions you should be asking."

He took a step closer, and I took a step back. Smiling, he reached out to trail long sharp nails along my cheek. His face remained in the dark while those empty eyes stared back at me.

"Sometimes, every little piece just falls into place, and it hangs in a precipice between good and evil."

"And I assume I'm that piece?"

He chuckled and trailed his nail across my neck. "No, hellhound. She is. Now finish your job and offer her what I'm giving."

"And what is that?"

"The sweetest of evils."

A heavy silence filled the night as he disappeared. Even the screams went quiet.

My hellhound stirred, knowing what I needed, and I let it take over. The echo of my bones breaking was unworldly. The pain was almost healing. I let it overcome me, held onto it. Held onto my own screams as he tore my flesh apart and I became his vessel. And I embraced the freedom that came with it. I wondered if my soul could ever break free this way. To say I'd miss the hellhound was an understatement. He was a part of me and I, a part of him.

I held on as he galloped through the shadows. Allowed myself to see the world through his eyes. It was rare when I allowed this for myself. But tonight, I needed it. I needed to feel something.

Anything.

It only took him a few hours before he brought us to the one place that I knew we should avoid. He leapt up onto the scaffolding. Going up to that fourth floor where her apartment lay. And then we both sat there and watched over her sleeping form. A sense of peace coming over us just knowing she was safe.

Hellhounds are used for two things. To guard the gates of hell, and as servants to the Dark Prince in carrying out his evil deeds. Never to protect a human. And as I sat there, beside my hellhound, I knew something was very, very wrong.

Elora

CHAPTER SEVENTEEN

**"The realm of gods & demons...are of the
substance of dreams."
~Joseph Campbell~**

My heart, beat erratically, my palms were sweaty, my eyes blurred. I searched the dense forest, unable to see what hunted me. I held the iron blade tightly in my hand, swinging it around me as I continued to scan my surroundings.

This dream was nothing like the ones where Beau and I met. This one was meant to ignite fear. I'd let my guard down with Beau, and I realized I'd let my focus wane. In the end, Beau was a predator, and I was his prey. One of us would eventually surrender, and in doing so, blood would spill.

I could sense whatever beast was out there, watching me.

"Come out!"

I instigated it, my hand shaking as I o7held the blade in front of my face.

"Show yourself!"

I startled as the howl of a hellhound echoed around me. Not thinking, I took off running. This wasn't Beau, it couldn't be Beau.

Why not?

That soft whisper in my subconscious sent my heart racing and I struggled to run faster. The cracking of twigs echoed all around me and I could hear the animal's harsh breath at my ear.

Run.

It was the only thought that kept replaying in my head. I had to run. Run far away where no one could find me, where nothing could touch me. The clouds grew overhead, blocking out the sun and graying the sky.

"Elora!"

"Momma?"

"Come home, Elora. I miss you."

I was suddenly watching my mom in the kitchen. The phone pressed to her ear as she begged me to come home. I always came back to this moment. Thinking that maybe if I had been home that night, and not running away from everything and everyone, that I could have been here to save her.

My heart broke as I watched her tears fall. I loved her more than life itself. Falling to my knees, I sobbed with her.

"She suffers because of you."

My eyes flew up as Ashdemai appeared in the kitchen, standing beside my mother as he petted her head.

"Don't touch her!"

He smiled, in that malevolent way of his, and continued to do as he pleased.

"She continues to cry for you with every day that passes. For all eternity," he chuckled.

I watched him as he continued to run his hands through her hair.

"If you give up your soul, maybe we can come to an agreement of some sort."

"Fuck you."

"Oh, well that's not nice."

"I know you well enough to know you like manipulating the truth to fill your twisted needs."

"Is that right?"

His hand drew down to the knife my mother had been using to chop vegetables.

"So you honestly believe your true and loyal mother is up in the heavens with those detested angels?"

I became overwhelmed with doubt. My mother had been good. She had lived her life as best as she knew how.

"My mother was good."

"No one is without sin, Elora. Not even you."

"If that were the case, then all humanity would be damned."

"But it's not all of humanity my dark lord is after, now, is it?"

He flipped the knife, the blade now pressed against my mother's neck.

"You can't hurt her."

He smiled, leaning down to whisper something in her ear. Suddenly her eyes flew up to mine.

"Elora?"

"Mom?"

"Your mother should have never played with that kind of black magic, Elora. She should have known better."

"No," I tried reaching for her but couldn't move. I was paralyzed.

"Don't you give in, Elora. Don't let him win."

I froze, my heart hurt hearing those words again. Those were the last words she ever said to me before she died.

"Your mother was a sweet kill. She only wept for her child. See, the one thing your mother didn't know was that by playing with darkness it made her such a delectable target."

"No." I shook my head in horror.

"No amount of protection spells would save her. She let the darkness in, Elora."

"No."

"And we don't play well with others."

"Please," I begged.

"She shouldn't have gotten in our way, Elora. My lord doesn't like that."

"Don't hurt her."

"Is that how you begged your Hellhound?"

"What? No." Confusion started to set in.

"Making him take you. Begging him to touch that dirty cunt of yours. Making him your dog!"

"No!"

"Well, your mother did just that, didn't she? She chained him up and took what didn't belong to her. And because of that, she paid a heavy price."

"I don't understand."

"No, of course not. You're too busy desiring things that aren't yours."

He pressed the tip of the blade into her skin, breaking flesh as a drop of blood emerged.

"That's not true!"

"The more you dig, the more you'll find that there are consequences that come from tampering with black magic."

"No."

"Gruesome consequences."

"No!" I reached out just as with a quick flick of his wrist, the blade slit through flesh and muscle.

A scream of terror ripped out of me, as my mother's eyes went blank and Ashdemai's evil laughter filled my head.

My body jolted in the bed. Sweat dripped down my back as I kicked off the sheets that had twisted around my ankles. I curled my legs up beneath me, as the clock stared back at me. The devil's hour was haunting me.

My mother's blank stare stayed with me as I stumbled into the bathroom, gripping onto the edge of the sink as I found my breath again. I looked up into the mirror and a tear fell down my cheek. My dark hair was matted to my forehead, the long t-shirt, with the logo of my favorite rock bands, was soaked in sweat. I tore it off me and stood there naked, in just my panties. I had scratch marks on my breasts and arms, something I didn't have before. And right along my neck, a red welt had formed.

I slid my fingertips along the bruise and started to shake. My legs collapsed from under me, and I crumbled to the floor. My hand gripped the sink as I pressed my forehead to it, letting out the sobs that I had kept in for years.

In the back of my head, my mother's words kept repeating like a mantra. It was as if she was given one last chance to repeat those words. And in them, I gathered strength.

Don't give in, Elora.

Don't let them win.

Beau

CHAPTER EIGHTEEN

An Enigmatic Agreement

I needed to feel her. I wanted her, but for my own sanity, I forced myself to stay away. She was a mark, that was all. At least that's what I kept telling myself, meanwhile I continued to grow desperate. It had all come together in one night. Lucifer was using Ashdemai, and the Sin was using his little mind tricks on us to manipulate and taunt us with what we couldn't have. He wanted us both to fall for his lust-filled antics, and if we did, I knew it would destroy us both. What a perfect ending that would be.

I want to go to her.

"We can't."

Why not?

"I don't fucking know!" I screamed, flinging the book I held in my hand against the television screen. A deep crack was now embedded in it, and I cursed.

I'd locked myself up in this dingy apartment for the last

week. The soul that used to occupy it was now gone and no one had even cared enough to clear his living space. It was far enough away from Elora that I stayed, and near enough that if she needed me, I'd be there in a heartbeat.

This can't go on forever. You can't hide from her.

"That's not what I'm doing."

That's exactly what you're doing.

The Hellhound went silent for a little while and when he questioned me, I knew he was phishing in my head for answers. Answers I didn't want to give.

Why did Lucifer send Ashdemai?

"For the girl."

You're going to have to give me a little bit more than that.

His angry growl filled my head, and I began to pace.

"Fine. Ashdemai has control of my dreams. In them, he's made me vulnerable to her...primal needs."

Lust.

"Yes."

Well that explains that. But it doesn't explain our need to protect her.

"No. I believe that's her mother's doing, and Lucifer seems to have some sort of vindication against her for it. Her mother used his own demons against him so he's looking for payback."

How?

"Through instigating lust, he is forcing the virgin to sin. Hence making her fall. But the spell is powerful enough that it seems we've become her protectors."

We're being pushed and pulled to do what they want, what do you want to do, Beau?

The question came out of nowhere. We both knew deep inside what we had to do to survive. Ashdemai had planted the suggestion in me and in her but not in the hellhound.

"I'm corrupted. I don't know if what I feel for her comes from the spell or from lust."

And what is that you feel?

"You're not going to believe me when I say this."

I've been through much more than you ever have. I'll believe anything at this point.

"I can feel my soul when I'm with her."

He went quiet for a long time. *You're not just being blinded by lust?*

"No. Yes. I don't know," I tugged on my hair, desperation rolling through me in waves.

It seems this is what Lucifer wanted. To cause chaos in you until you made the decision that would benefit him. You're at a crossroads. Give into your lust and you damn her to sin, if you go against his wishes, you damn yourself to an eternity of pain.

"There has to be another way."

Don't you get it, human. She's the way. She's the only way.

"She's going to kill us both, Hellhound."

If this is what the fates want, there's really nothing we can do about it.

Acheron slid another *Corpse Reviver* my way as soon as I sat down.

"I don't know how you can down those. They must taste like acid."

I shrugged. "Just habit, I guess. It feels warm as it goes down."

Acheron shrugged. "At least there's some comfort in it. Can't stomach the stuff."

"Because you took too much pleasure in it when alive."

"And enough pain," he muttered under his breath.

We each had our punishment in death, and it came in various ways. For Acheron, one of those ways was the drink, which had led to his death. Gluttony had come down and chosen him for ruination, and his state of depression, he must have been an easy target. Now, if Acheron touched the thing, it would burn his insides, yet he was condemned to exist around it for eternity.

"Lucifer sure does have a sense of humor. Don't you think so, Beau?"

I turned my head toward the voice that came from the entity seated at the end of the bar. The tattoos on his forearms signaled he wasn't a hellhound. This entity entered hell by his own means.

"Kimaris," I growled.

My hellhound wasn't as fond of fallen angels as you would think. These angels walked among the humans once, taking the fall in order to experience life. Their punishment would be to serve Lucifer for all of eternity. Half of them were influenced by demons, the other half made their choice which made them dangerous. They turned their back on God, and for that alone, they were not meant to be trusted.

Kimaris was an angel. He was one of the Fallen who didn't quite make it to the title of Prince of Hell. See, he didn't come to Lucifer's battles, he came with his own agenda.

"Haven't seen you around here in years. What brings you back?" Acheron questioned him, the tension between them palpable.

"Relax, dog. I did not come here for you."

I kept my head down during their exchange, avoiding

any trouble. Having a fallen angel on your trail was never a good sign.

I could feel his eyes on me, and I slowly turned my head toward him.

"Who sent you, Kimaris?"

"The rumor is that you've lost something."

The grip on the glass in my hand tightened. "I don't know what you've heard, but I haven't lost a thing."

"Maybe not. But your hellhound can't say the same."

My hound snarled and dragged his paws as if preparing for a fight.

I'll kill him.

His whisper made Kimaris grin. "He's a feisty one, isn't he?"

"I doubt you want to instigate him."

"I thought you had a handle on your hellhound?"

"Doesn't make him any less powerful. And besides, don't ever forget he's got a mind of his own." I looked down at my drink and grinned. "If he wants to tear your wings apart, who am I to stop him?"

"There's really no need for violence. I came here offering my services."

I turned in my stool to face him. "We don't need any help."

"I hear you have one more soul left, and she's giving you a bit of trouble."

"Possibly. What's it to you?"

"Just wanting to help."

"Why?" Acheron asked, his eyes narrowing on him.

"Let's just say, I too wasn't given what was promised."

Acheron glanced at me and raised a brow. We didn't trust demons easily let alone fallen angels. They all came with their own ulterior motives that weren't worth anybody's while.

"Do you take me for a fool? As if I don't know you want something else from me. Who sent you, Kimaris?"

"Listen, I can understand you don't trust me. But there is someone out there who requested my help, I saw a window of opportunity and I took it."

"Who sent you?" I insisted.

"I can't tell you that. The walls have ears," he gestured to several demons who were mulling around among the living. "But what I can say is that if I help you, it may lead me to where my mark lies."

"I didn't realize angels had marks." Acheron smirked.

"We don't, but this one was not meant to be a mark. She became one because of me."

"Kimaris, you are known for helping at a hefty price." I leaned toward him, lowering my tone. "So, name it."

"Access to hell's gates."

Acheron and I looked at one another and we both let out a howl of laughter.

"I swear you fallen angels are just asking for it. Aren't you bound to purgatory."

"What I require is within those gates."

"And what makes you think I can get you in."

"You can't. But your hellhound can."

Fuck that.

I smirked as my hound cursed. "He's not very fond of you."

"Nor I of him. But he damn well knows that if you're gone, he has no vessel and no protection. His destruction is imminent."

"You don't know that.

"Lucifer will not keep his promise. And even if he did,

the hellhound has his own debts to pay. Isn't that right, Hellhound?"

End this. I could feel the hellhound's aggravation.

"This is the first time Lucifer has had to actually go through with it," Acheron whispered.

"And he'll do everything in his power to make you lose," Kimaris added. "See, if you win, he loses face. And the Dark Lord will have none of that."

He's not as crazy as I thought he was.

"Now you're agreeing with him?" I whispered.

It's not as if he's bringing up something we didn't know.

My hound stirred and began to pace.

"If he doesn't let you win, what makes you think he cares for a troublesome hellhound?"

The hellhound growled and I allowed him to speak for himself. I started to sweat as I lowered my head. He made the slight transition as easy as possible, so as not to alert the humans that mulled around us.

My fangs protruded, hair grew thicker on the back of my hands in cohesion with my nails, which became claw like. The hair on my head slowly grew out to my shoulders and when I looked up, my eyes glowed red.

In this form we became one, and the hound was allowed to use his vessel to speak while I still held control. It was something we rarely did.

"Speak."

My voice held that growly, guttural sound, and the intent behind his order held enough force to issue a warning. In this state my senses heightened. I could hear how Kimaris bit down on his molars, and I could smell the musk of sweat that came from him, signaling to me that he wasn't as confident as he seemed.

"It's good to see you again, Hellhound."

"Make it quick Kimaris. I have no patience for suicide missions."

He smirked. "You remind me of that stubborn vessel of yours."

"He's not without his good qualities. Now talk."

"I can help you both."

"And what do you want from me?"

"I need a guide to take me down."

"You think a fallen angel can walk freely in the infernal region?"

"Yes. As long as I become a hellhound's vessel."

"What makes you think I won't tear you apart?"

"I don't. All I know is that you don't have anything to lose?"

Is it true, will you be destroyed? I asked him.

He hesitated, and then I caught him give me a quick nod in the reflection in the mirror across from us.

Then do it.

He frowned in the mirror. His eyes glowing brighter.

I can only protect you until I get my last soul. And that's exactly what I plan to do. Even if you don't trust him, he's right. You can be free.

I waited, knowing what his answer was going to be but not wanting to give it. Instead, he released me, and slowly morphed us back so I was speaking.

"Does he not want my help?" Kimaris looked at me, anxiously waiting for my response.

I nodded. "He'll take it. But if you betray him, I will make it my life's mission to destroy you."

"I've never seen such loyalty."

"He got me my freedom, it's a debt I owe him."

You've kept me existing. You owe me nothing.

I ignored him, waiting on Kimaris.

"Then let's get you a soul." He banged his hand on the table in satisfaction.

I caught Acheron's hesitation. He wasn't convinced.

"Watch your back, Beau. Everyone here is servicing their own agenda."

I downed my last reviver and tipped the glass upside down on the bar top in front of me.

"Then I might as well get my own. Let's just say I'm tired of wearing a leash."

"I wish you luck, friend."

"Luck is the least I'll need."

I needed a goddamn miracle.

Turning to Kimaris, I walked up to him. "Do you know where her soul is?"

"I have an idea."

"What do you know?"

"Black magic was in the works here."

I nodded. "That's pretty clear. What else?"

"There's word of a spell where a soul can be bound to another. Not anyone can use that spell. Blood needs to be spilled, and a life must be taken."

It suddenly crossed my mind that there was more to Elora's mother's death than met the eye. She would do anything to keep her daughter safe. And I wouldn't put it past her, to give her life for her daughter's.

"What happens if that life is taken?"

"Then that soul finds the other, and they become inseparable. So much so that they will go through several lives trying to find one another."

"Soul mates," I scoffed.

"More powerful. They say a twin flame is so powerful it can feel its kindred spirit to the point of suffering."

I simply stared at him, trying to assimilate what he was

saying and what I was now feeling for Elora. I needed to get out of there. Clear my mind and figure out what it was that was happening between her and I.

"I will call you when I need you."

"Just make sure you do it before they find it. Rumors spread quickly, and Lucifer has no patience. She's kept her soul well hidden, and he will stop nothing to get his payment. I won't be able to help you if he or Ashdemai find it first."

"I won't need you to find it, Angel. I need you to protect it until I figure out what to do with it."

"The answer should be simple. He owns her."

"Not yet. I have a feeling she remains alive for a reason. Give me some time. I'll call you when I need you."

I lifted the collar of my black overcoat as I stepped out into the cold brisk winter. It has begun to snow in New York, and as I made my way to my post at her window, my mind was spinning, and my heart had somehow begun to beat once again.

Elora

CHAPTER NINETEEN

Bane & Bound

I opened the store as usual, tending to customers and helping with any questions that arose. Customers came in for all sorts of spells, others for books, and yet others came in search for herbs that cured ails. Karma was busy in the back counting inventory.

I liked busy days; it made time go by a lot faster and I didn't have to think. They were a blessing in their own way, even though time was precious, and I should use it to my advantage.

It wasn't until the end of the day, when I was sitting alone in my office, that I thought back on my dream and on the hellhound and his vessel that had suddenly disappeared.

I wondered if something had happened to him or if he was hurt. Such a stupid notion. A human worrying over a hellhound. I should be grateful he had left me at peace for a while. I hadn't felt this sort of quiet in a long time.

I walked out to the store, which had a dim emergency light on in the entrance. I walked past the bookshelf and noticed the dark magic book open on the table. I stared at it for a second wondering if I had ever put it away last night after doing my research.

It was obvious my mother had to spill her own blood to make this work, but was it at the cost of her life, as Ashmedai had so cruelly put it. He was master at manipulating your desires, and dreams were desires unknown.

I touched the corner of the book, feeling its power trying to pull me in. I put up another wall and shoved the energy away. It knew how to use its magic to corrupt you. And if you were weak to it, you could fall into its grasp, like so many others have done before.

I didn't believe in soul mates, but my mother was of another thought. According to the spell she had used, it bound my soul to that of another's. I just needed to find out to whom, and there was only one way to do that.

Grabbing one of my mother's personal spell books, I closed the one with black magic and set it aside. I didn't practice magic, but I wasn't without the teachings of my mother. If I was going to search for someone, then I needed a few items. A candle, both black and white, tarot cards, obsidian stone on a silver chain, and water to cleanse the energy.

As soon as I had everything I needed, I lit the candle, setting it down beside the bowl of water. I closed my eyes and breathed as I began to shuffle the cards.

One. Two Three.

To the angels true and fallen
Guide my way
That I may be able to acquire
For which my soul is bound in bane
Take me to what has been lost
That I may find a way.
I invite you in, whoever you are, wherever you are,
Feel my energy and look for me.
Make yourself known to me and I to you.
May it harm none,
And as I ask this,
So mote it be.

I lay the first card on the table and nearly laughed. The Devil had the lovers chained to his will. The second card flew out, a Tower destroyed, the lovers thrown out of it. And then the last card was presented, the Eight of Swords. A woman sat there, with swords surrounding her, making her feel trapped and suffocated. I stared at the cards for a long time, and I finally asked my question.

"Is my soul trapped with his?"

The Sun appeared in the reading, guiding light and responding with a resounding, *yes*. I wondered what he looked like, and I laid another card down, continuing the reading with another question.

"What is his appearance?"

The Emperor flew out of my hand. He was an attractive leader, somewhat controlling.

I set the cards aside and grabbed the map with the obsidian stone. I lifted the chain, letting it hover among the Map of the Realms. Heaven and hell were prominent, so was purgatory, but there were levels and one of them was earth.

I raised the chain and asked the angels to procure the soul's location. The obsidian began to sway back and forth, back and forth, when suddenly a force knocked it out of my hand. I slid my chair back, slamming it against the bookshelf as a shadow appeared before me.

He came into the light of the candle and my eyes widened, as a silhouette of black wings spanned behind him. A fallen angel had heard my call.

"You'll never find him there."

His voice was low and gravelly, and he was a giant of a man, muscular and inked in sigils. His wings were black as midnight, and they fluttered behind him as he paced before me.

"You will not find your twin flame here."

"Who are you?"

"Kimaris."

My eyes widened, and my grip tightened on the protection amulet that dangled from my neck. Kimaris was a demon. A fallen angel that possessed the ability of locating hidden treasures. But he was evil in his own right, wielding a weapon that when fired, it would engulf its target in an endless void of darkness, causing sheer panic among humanity where the victim eventually goes mad, and suicide ensues.

"What does a fallen angel want with me?"

"Just as cynical as your hellhound."

"Beau? Where is he?"

"Alive and well and figuring out just what his desires are when they come to you."

He chuckled as I blushed, and he knew exactly what I wanted to know.

"Why are you here?"

"You summoned me."

"I summoned no demon."

"Angels true and fallen. I guess the true ones were busy." He curled his lip in an attempt at a smile, and I gave him a calculated look. He may be evil personified, but he had maintained his beauty even though he had been cast out of the heavens.

"I'll make this quick because there is no time. I made a promise that I'd find you, and since we have this opportunity then I'll seize it. Your soul has been bound, and its location is somewhere between purgatory and hell."

"My soul is lost?"

"For now. It seems the fates and a powerful spell have interfered in Lucifer's plans."

"They can do that?"

"They can do that and much more. The fates exist for everyone, Elora. Both humans and demons. If they can get in between heaven and hell, they will."

"There is an in between?"

"There are many in betweens, Elora."

"How do I get to it?"

"I want to make one thing clear; a twin flame is not one you can separate from. Your mother may not have known what she did when she spoke her incantation, but the fates have sealed your union. There is no way of undoing that type of edict."

"What do you mean?"

"Your mother bound your soul to none other than a man who has only one way out of hell."

My eyes widened. "Beau," I breathed his name.

Kimaris watched me beneath his dark hooded lashes.

"You're his only way out, Elora. If he falls, you fall with him."

"That's ridiculous. He has a hellhound inside of him. A demon! I could never be one with such a reprobate."

"You have no choice."

Thunder struck nearby and I jolted in my seat, reality slowly sinking in. Kimaris smiled down at me. "I'll take my leave now. I'm sure we'll see each other again."

"Wait!" He paused, turning to look at me over his wings.

"What happens if I fall first?"

He shrugged. "Taking chances is what life is all about, isn't it. Just be careful. I took a chance once and look where that got me."

Before I could ask him anything else, he faded into the darkness, taking the light of the candle with him.

Beau

Love is just an Illusion

The dream had pulled me into an infinite black hole. Wandering the outskirts of hell was not a pleasant experience, especially when the wails of the dead reached you.

Then there were the lost blessed souls who reached out to you on either side of that treacherous path. One misstep and the souls would grab you, dragging you in with them. One slip and you'd go tumbling into that vast ditch, swallowed by the heavy darkness. The sobs of lament and agony resonating in a never-ending plea, as those who once loved you, abandoned you.

I was alone on this path of misery, my hellhound long forgotten. I continued to trudge on, the fog slowly clearing as ahead I heard a familiar whimper. I struggled to see through the smoky fog, but I knew it was her voice.

I tripped on my own two feet, catching myself before I

was lunged into that abyss. I scrambled to get up, becoming frantic in my search for her as I followed her voice.

I saw her in the distance, my legs not long enough, my feet not fast enough to get to her. As I reached for her, I was suddenly jerked back and lifted off my feet. I was being forced to watch Elora as she was struck over and over again.

Demons stood at either side of her while she hung on a saltire cross, arms and legs bound to that X. Her naked figure exposed. I tried to blink it away, shake my head and cry out to my hellhound to wake me up, but there was no escaping this.

Lucifer was forcing this on me, and I was demanded to sit still and watch.

I struggled against the hold they had on me, and a demon came over to me. Her eyes glowed that familiar red as a serpent slivered out of her mouth. She eyed me, and when she smiled, sharp teeth greeting me. Her hand slithered up my leg and onto my crotch, and I froze.

"My Dark Lord has plans for you both. Trust me, you don't want to miss thissss..." She hissed out the words as she turned toward the sight before us.

"Beau!" Elora cried for me as the demons each took their chance at whipping her with steel tipped leather straps. Each slash tore through my clothes and onto my flesh.

Her body trembled erotically as she undulated against the cross. I couldn't help but to desire her. Disgusting, I know, but yet I loved to see her body sway and jolt with each powerful switch of the strap.

Another lash, another cry of pain from her, yet I was the one whose flesh was torn. The demon beside me cackled as she rubbed my now hardened length.

"She's beautiful, isn't she? Prime to be devoured, her virginity yours for the taking."

A leather strap slid across her breasts, curling around her taut nipple like a tentacle and I watched as her body jerked off the cross, quivering in fear while my flesh burned from the lashing. I grew hard, engulfed by that primal need to make her mine.

I yelled out, cursing at the devil, begging to be released, but he was enjoying the cruelty he'd created. Making it known that this would be our ceaseless punishment. A yearning never fulfilled.

"I will never let you have her!"

Another lashing struck me along my torso, the burn lingering. When I looked down, my body was being torn to pieces. Flesh hung from bone, and blood pooled on the tar ridden floor below me.

"She belongs to the Fallen One. Dare you to deceive your master?"

I looked down at the demon with one word on my tongue. "Yes."

The demon seemed stunned by my admonition, and she hissed back as she didn't dare to touch me.

The Hellhound was right, there is only thing more powerful than lust.

Love.

I looked up at Elora whose eyes looked tired and devastated and something in me knew I was meant to protect her. Everything I'd done up to this point led up to this. Whether it was the fates, gods, or devils and their demons, a twin flame, a soulmate, none of it mattered. One thing was real to me among all that lore. Elora was a part of me, and in so being, I belonged to her.

As soon as I realized this, I was released. It took me a second to realize I was no longer being held back, and I scrambled to my feet, staggering forward as the lashings on her continued. Just as I lay my hands on her, a scream tore through the wails of the dead, and the earth beneath my feet began to shatter. I lost my balance, and as I was flung back into that abyss, I was jerked out of my nightmare.

I found myself running at full speed, using the shadows to take long leaps through the air.

"What's going on!" I screamed to the hellhound as he galloped through the streets, his sense of frenzy had taken over.

Elora.

I could sense she was frightened by something, and I cursed at myself for not being there when she needed me.

You disappeared again. Your empty vessel was left behind.

"It's fine. You did what you had to do."

I realized that he may have even saved my life at that moment. I was grateful for him watching over me. And I'd be damned if I didn't find a way to repay him.

We entered quietly, like a loyal watchful dog he paced around the protection circle which kept her safe. He tensed as her body rose, her hands gripping the sheets until her fists grew white.

He's hurting her.

The hellhound leapt on top of her. Nudging her and whining, not knowing what to do. She suddenly screamed my name, and I could feel her agonized fright.

The hellhound snarled, bending down and biting down around her neck, just enough to cause her to jolt awake. He instantly pulled away as she shoved herself against the headboard.

"Beau?"

My name on her lips broke my heart and my hellhound slowly backed off allowing me to comfort her.

Elora

Sweet Innocence

I'd wanted to go to bed early tonight. I'd been thinking of him the entire day, and that usually ended with me alone, in bed, imagining him between my legs. I was so exhausted I must have fallen asleep, and in doing so, I fell into a nightmare I couldn't get out of.

I was being chased, but not by the hellhound or the man, this was an entity I hadn't encountered before. It hid in the darkness, a malevolent intent in its energy. It was chasing me along desolate streets. It didn't matter where I ran to, it was there, hovering over me, feeding off my fear.

I was at a dead end, searching for a way out. And that's when I felt its decrepit, cold fingers close around my throat, slowly suffocating me. I screamed the only name that came to mind. And I hoped with all my heart that my agony would finally end, and my fate would be sealed.

I was lost in the dream when I was suddenly jerked

awake. As if pulled from beneath its hold. The hellhound was crouched above me, that red-eyed glow piercing the darkness. Sniffing me, it snarled, its snout pulling back and baring sharp teeth.

I gasped, rearing back toward the headboard. Attempting to escape it, but there's no escaping this type of predator.

"Beau?" I asked it, and it snarled at me again.

Shaking its head back and forth, its fur quivering as though it were struggling within itself. Wide-eyed, I watched as his form changed. His eyes turned an amber hue, his snout became a hard chiseled jawline, the black fur became a full beard, closely trimmed.

His body arched back as the hound retreated, and I lay there dumbfounded yet fascinated as Beau's naked form came into view. Broad chest, tight muscles that flexed as they strained over well-defined tendons, thick strong thighs spread wide as he knelt before me. My eyes fell between them, where his cock jutted out. Long and hard, a thick mushroom head with pulsating veins that curled around its base. It looked angry. It looked dangerous. My core clenched from the sight of it. If these feelings of lust were truly full of sin, why in the fuck did they feel so good.

"Beau?" I whispered his name once again, unsure of who the man in my bedroom was.

He slowly lifted his eyes to me. The flames of the hound came to the surface, and he licked his lips.

"I can smell your arousal, Elora."

"Why are you here?"

"You called me."

I shook my head, remembering how I had screamed his name in my dream.

"You heard me?"

"We both felt you."

He leaned forward, crawling toward me.

"Don't."

His eyes said it all as he reached for me.

"You're scared."

"I'm fine."

His hand caressed my hair and I swallowed nervously. I'd never been touched in a caring way, not by a man, least of all a demon. I wasn't sure how to react.

"That seductive scent engulfs me."

"It was just a nightmare. You should go."

"Don't lie to me, Elora. I can hear how fast your heart is beating. You were scared."

"What if I was? I thought you'd enjoy that."

"You're wrong," his voice lowered.

I narrowed my eyes on him. "What do you want, Beau?"

"I want you," his voice was rough, almost strained.

"Well, I don't want you anywhere near me. You can go. Go back to the hell you came from, just pretend I never existed."

"As if it were that easy."

"Isn't it? You've been able to stay away from me so far."

"And that bothered you?"

"Trust me. You're already kept in the far recesses of my mind. You mean nothing to me."

"Don't lie to me!"

I gasped as calloused fingers ran up my legs, roughly ripping them apart.

"Beau!" I tried to push him away.

"I want you, Elora. I want your scent all over me and mine all over you."

"Don't, Beau."

His hands slid up my thighs, and I shook in that damn yearning that came with more.

"I said don't!"

I watched this dark beast of a man crawl between my thighs. The entire time, I was half paralyzed in terror and half mesmerized with how darkly beautiful he was. I had no recognition of time or space. The world just stopped as he leaned forward, touching me so gently.

So seductive.

"Your arousal calls out to us," he said, his voice deceptively soft as he trailed his roughened fingertips along the seam of my pussy.

"You were playing with it before we arrived."

I bit my lip, avoiding the consequences that would come with my response.

"Answer me!" He slapped my inner thigh, and I cried out.

"Y-yes!" My lips trembled as I watched him dip his head, pressing his nose to my mound, and inhaling me. I writhed beneath him, as the brush of his coarse beard against my soft flesh elicited dark and sinful feelings in me.

"Were you thinking of me?"

"No."

His hand cracked harder against my inner thigh, and I jumped.

"Liars get punished, Elora."

"Does it matter?"

"Ohhh, it matters," he growled, gripping my hips, and yanking me down until my head hit the mattress.

He swept a tendril of my hair aside, caressing my cheek so tenderly it caught me off guard.

"I'm living in this chaos that you've provoked. Do you think that's fair?"

I wasn't sure how to respond, nor did I know what he wanted to hear. None of this was fair to either of us. Neither was this pull he had on me. It was maddening.

I managed a weak response. "I don't know."

"What don't you know, Elora?"

I shook my head, my body trembling beneath his. "I-I just don't know."

His eyes glowed brightly as they grazed my body. His hands traced a heated path where his eyes settled, hovering lightly over my breasts until my nipples hardened beneath the thin nightgown.

"You don't know if you want to be fucked?"

I whimpered as my eyes glazed over a little. "I never said that."

"You don't know if you want me to make you my dirty little whore?"

I gasped as his hand fisted the hem of my nightgown, yanking it up, over my waist. His calloused fingertips grazed the bare skin above the waistband of my panties. My stomach dipped and quivered beneath that feather-light touch.

"You don't know if you want me to make you do things you've never done before?" He asked.

"Beau," his name slipped out in the form of a plea.

I was begging him; I just didn't know what for.

"Do you want to feel my dick pulsing inside you? Fucking this sweet virgin pussy, hard and deep?"

"Oh, God!" My thighs trembled as I fought to keep from reaching for him.

"Want me to use you however I please and just make you take it?" he asked, his voice so dark and deep, so... forbidden.

"We can smell your need for me," he growled. His voice a gruff echo, traced in the hound's heat.

Gripping the seams of my panties, he tore at them with such vicious haste that I barely registered what was happening until I felt his hot breath on my core.

He snarled as his heated gaze locked on my pussy, feeling open and slick with my cream from coming so hard a few hours before.

"Such a pretty little cunt." He stroked my clit, and I gasped as my body trembled with need. "I like that it's bare and I can see everything."

"Please, don't," I begged. But my pleas fell on deaf ears.

Ashdemai had taken his suggestive grip on us and he was coiling his lustful tentacles around our weak and fragile necks.

"My hellhound wants a taste of you. His tongue is longer than mine. Rougher too. I'm going to fuck this pretty little cunt with my hound's tongue, and you're going to let us."

His words were perverse, yet they aroused me so severely I could barely breathe. They were laced with the dirtiest of sins and I was fighting with myself to reject him, even though all I wanted was to give in.

I don't know when he began to shift. But I could feel the dip of his sharp claws locking onto my thighs. He nicked me with his fangs, and I cried out as pain mixed with pleasure, and then he began to suck on me. Hard angry pulls that sent me into an unknown precipice. I whined from the feel of his coarse tongue lashing at my clit.

"Beau, noooo!" My rejection fell out as a needy moan all while his hot, wet tongue curled around my untouched clit. I shivered. His hungry moan mixed with a deep growl that came from the hellhound within him. I could feel the beast's arousal as it ate my pussy. It licked each lip, sucked on me in slow, hard pulls, slowly driving me crazy.

I fisted the sheets, spreading my thighs and lifting my hips to his mouth. My body writhed in shameful need.

He swirled his tongue across the bud, then plunged it deep inside my aching pussy. I cried out and felt my inner walls try to pull him deeper. He flicked his tongue in and out of me, and I'd have sworn it felt as if he were licking my wounds.

Beau pinned my thighs open, making it impossible for me to move, as he devoured my pussy. When I came, he kept rubbing my clit with his sandpaper-like tongue, and I nearly saw stars. I came again and again, wanting to cry from the intensity as he pulled one orgasm after another out of me.

When he lifted his head, his hand wrapped around my neck and held me still, those red glowing eyes watching me intently as he lashed his tongue against my nipples. They were so sensitive, that rough feeling alone made me nearly cum again. I felt mindless with my need for him, and I was seconds from begging him to fuck me. To really fuck me.

"It hurts," he murmured against my lips.

"What hurts?"

"This," he placed my hand over the mark on his chest and in unison I hissed from the heat, and he groaned.

"I need to mark you," he said, his voice the deep growl of his beast. "Make you mine."

"I can't allow that," I whispered.

"I don't require your permission."

He pressed his mouth to my ear. "I've never lost control of the hellhound before. Can you feel him? He wants to rut, to take you again and again, make you smell like us."

He leaned forward and grazed his fangs over my shoulder. That deep guttural voice was igniting every nerve in my body. "He wants to bite into this delicate skin and mark you as ours."

I slid my hands through his long dark hair. Tugging at it until his eyes fell on me. "If I fall, I'm dragging you down with me."

"Then fall," he growled, and I cried out as he bit down on my breast.

My orgasm was overpowering, the world spun, and everything started going dark. The last thing I felt was Beau wrapping his strong arms around me, holding me tight against his body, right before I passed out.

Beau

"The road to self-destruction is quick and swift."

The Hellhound was about to bind her to us before we'd been interrupted. Even a beast like me didn't fuck like a feral animal all the time. She'd made my basic urges come to the surface, and when she'd surrendered, I hadn't been able to hold back. Thinking of claiming her innocence had only unleashed the monster inside, and there was no coming back from that. She was undeniably mine. I knew I'd get another chance, but the hellhound that dwelled inside me wasn't happy that I'd forced him to wait.

His hellish temper rose, and he made it known how much he hated my guts.

You had one task!

"Which I am currently in the process of working out."

You've taken enough time.

"I haven't even begun!" I seethed.

I paced the apartment I had taken as my own. Old magic and demonology books I had taken from the library were strewn everywhere. I couldn't find anything on what to do to save her soul, let alone my own. I slumped down in the middle of the living room, my back against the couch, as a figure appeared before me.

When I looked up, I grimaced. "Haven't you done enough?"

"Not quite."

Ashdemai scanned the small space and then shook his head. "I never understood how humanity can live in such condensed chaos."

"It's a source of comfort."

"Vessels are not allowed to do any such thing."

"I'm not just any vessel."

He crouched down before me, wearing that perfectly pressed navy-blue business suit. He looked put together, a complete contrast to the burning remnants of his face. He smelled of burning sulfur, a putrid smell, much unlike the smell of brimstone the hellhounds tended to emanate.

"I know what games you're playing, Beau. I can smell her on you. From what it looks like, you can't keep your dick in your pants nor your dog under control."

"I'm sure you're enjoying the show."

"Not in the least bit. End the fucking torture already. What are you waiting for? You have one more mark, and you are going to blow it over some pussy."

I chuckled. "You're only mad because I haven't fallen victim to your designs."

"It's only a matter of time."

"Don't underestimate me, demon."

"All I see is self-destruction. You've never cared a day about anyone but yourself. She's just another hole to fuck.

You can't fill your void this way. The only way to do that is to get your soul back."

"You think I don't want that!"

"No one's stopping you but you, Beau."

He chuckled as I took a drink of the bitter drink which dangled from my fingertips. I did my best to remember the living. To remember their tastes, their luxuries, their irrelevant need for attention and acceptance. I hadn't felt anything in all these years. Nothing tangible. Yet I could still feel her soft flesh beneath my fingertips and the taste of her on my tongue. I didn't want to let that go. I've spent a century alone. A partner in life hadn't existed, and it never came to mind as I served Lucifer throughout the years. But I could say one this, no one has ever compared to her. No one has ever stirred up this amount of pain and turmoil in me as this one human woman has. That had to mean something.

"Lucifer will get his soul when he gets his soul."

"Either you take her soul, or I will. Humans are susceptible to so many wicked things. I just need to find the right one."

"It's you, isn't it? The one causing her nightmares."

He smirked. "Somebody had to scare some sense into her."

Throwing my glass out of the way, I grabbed at the lapels of his suit, bringing him down to my level. "If you touch her, I will make it my endless mission to make you suffer."

Ashdemai marred lip curled. "I love the taste of Wrath. She has a powerfully intoxicating way about her, doesn't she? I may pay her a visit. I do miss her."

"Fuck you," I shoved him off me.

"A hellhound protecting a human. I'd heard rumors but never expected them to be true. You're no angel,

Kavanaugh, you're just a lowly vessel who has been given an order and you will obey your master."

"He has never been my master!"

My hellhound snarled back at him. Ashdemai paused for a second before his own snarl echoed in my head, staggering me back.

"And keep that dog on a fucking leash. As soon as you're gone, he's gone. Don't fucking forget that."

They don't know.

The hellhound whispered.

"Nor will they."

Ashmedai had no idea that Elora's soul was missing. It seemed Lucifer didn't know either, if not he wouldn't be urging me to bring it to him. Ashdemai had given himself away. Which meant he had no knowledge of Kimaris. The advantage of being a fallen angel was that they could walk among the living or the dead unseen, that included demons.

"The less they know, the more time we have."

I can sense when she's in danger. We must stay by her side.

"Don't you get it, Hellhound. I'm the danger. If you allow me anywhere near her, I'll ruin her."

Is that such a bad thing?

"Yes!"

Only if you allow it to become what they want.

"Lust is a sexual obsession."

Yet without it, love wouldn't exist.

I chuckled. "Manipulations really are a demon's gift."

I am not manipulating you, but just think about it. Not only are you lusting after her, you seek to protect her. Would you give your soul up for hers, human?

"What are you talking about?"

You're treading on treacherous waters, Beau Kavanaugh. You are running away from the obvious truth.

I slammed my fist against the floor in frustration. "And what is the goddamned truth to you?"

I'm not the one you should be asking, human. Take a look at yourself, at what you've become. The answer is there, you just need to open your eyes.

"Yeah well, I haven't spotted it even with your all-powerful senses."

I felt the hound shake and stretch as it curled up in itself.

I'll leave the thinking up to you. Just know that the more you avoid the feeling, the more you'll suffer.

Deep inside I knew what he was hinting at, but that was impossible.

Love was nonexistent, a mere primal instinct that was only heightened by lust. Love was a myth. Just like everything that surrounded it. In the last century, I'd only seen it cause violence, and betrayals, tears full of heartache.

I looked up to the sky, and smirked. "Keep your lousy love. I don't want it. It's all a lie, just like you."

Throwing my head back against the cushions, I closed my eyes. My entire being was in tune with hers now. I could feel her from the tips of my fingers to the head of my cock. Her body stretched out and mine stretched with hers. If she was angry, I became wrath, if she was needy, I became lust, and if she was lost, I was lost without her. The connection had only gotten more powerful with our last interaction, and I continued to go down a dark frenzied path, with only one end in sight. One that only offered destruction and sorrow.

Beau

CHAPTER TWENTY-THREE

A Wicked Game of Seduction

I made my way back to that hole in the wall I now called a home. It was hidden in a seedy location, perfect for a hellhound to dwell in his sorrows and in the soul he lost.

I entered through the bedroom window, what had now become a normal routine. But tonight, the atmosphere had changed and as I landed on one knee, an arm wrapped around my neck and the cold hard planes of a steel blade slid along my throat.

I smiled, silently applauding her for catching me off guard.

"Don't move," she whispered in my ear.

"Who's the stalker now?"

She tightened her arm's grip on me. Pulling me up against her plush tits.

"You should have told me this is what it took to have you pressed against me."

"It would be so easy to slit your throat."

"Then do it." I urged her.

"Put us both out of our misery."

She drew long steady breaths against my neck. My eyes angled down towards her hand, as she drew it out, the tip of the blade pressed on my jugular.

"Do it, Elora."

Her hand shook and her breathing hardened. "I can't " she released me, the blade clattering against the floorboards.

I turned swiftly. Lifting her around the waist and slamming us against the nearest wall. I was livid, but in the midst of my anger, a sense of relief filled me. Because she was back in my arms where she belonged.

"How did you find me?"

"Your hellhound is not the only one who knows how to track."

I let out a low growl and squeezed her tightly to me. "You shouldn't have come."

"Why not?" I jerked back slightly as her hands came up to gently touch my face.

"What are you doing, Elora?"

"I'm not sure."

"Yes, you are. You're stirring the beast."

"Were you a good man? In life?"

Her question took me by surprise. "Does it matter?"

She shrugged. "Maybe."

"I was a selfish prick who did drug and alcohol runs. Satisfied."

She shook her head. "I don't think that's completely true."

"No?" She was causing havoc on my senses. And that tender touch of her was making me lose all my defenses.

"I feel something else coming from you."

"What's that?"

"Fear."

Her eyes fixed on mine, and I grabbed her hands, shoving them off Mr.

"You know nothing."

"I know you were sent to kill me, and you haven't."

I bit down on my cheek, forcing myself to turn away.

"You don't know anything."

"I know my soul is lost and the hellhound of yours can't find it."

I gave out a short sarcastic laugh. "If that were true, every demon who had come looking for you would have found that out."

"Every demon who has come looking for me hasn't lived to tell the tale."

I turned back towards her, leaning into her until our noses touched.

"Why did you come looking for me?"

She hesitated for a long moment. And as she spoke, her voice cracked. "I'm tired, Beau."

Tears slid down her cheeks and my heart softened, so did my hellhound. He almost purred in longing. I reached out, softly wiping each salty drop away.

"Me too, Sweets. More than you know."

I continued to hold her pinned to that wall, even though she stopped fighting. Instead, I wanted to touch her, soothe her the only way I knew how. No matter what I told myself. I couldn't stay away. I didn't want to.

"Elora." Her name slipped off my tongue, traced in angst and need.

Her eyes met mine and I closed the distance between us. Allowing my kiss to speak for me. My hands acted on their own accord, slipping her leather jacket off her shoulders, and fighting with the hem of her sweatshirt as I nearly ripped it off her.

The hellhound groaned as her tits came into view, encased in a sheer black bra. I bent down. Putting my mouth over the fragile material, suckling on her breast in hard deep pulls.

"This is so wrong," she sighed while my tongue lapped at the hardened tips of her tits.

How I loved playing havoc on her senses. Watching her slowly submit to me was an aphrodisiac. One that made my cock hard and my mouth water.

"But it feels good, doesn't it, Elora? You feel good on the edge of that precipice. Do you want to fall with me?"

"No," shook her head from side to side, trying feebly to push me away. Failing miserably as I played her body like a fiddle.

That's what she was, a plaything for my demon. The devil's fiddle he could use as he pleased, and I was his bow, manipulated into strumming each crevice of her soft flesh.

I tugged her jeans down her legs. Her panties torn to shreds, disappearing into the recesses of the apartment.

I fell to my knees before her, and that lust-filled gaze fell on me. I lifted her leg up, perching her foot on a nearby chair. She looked lewd standing in the darkness with her leg raised and her thighs open, that sweet wet feminine candy being offered to her demon The moonlight played along her soft white flesh, highlighting her curves, making her look ghostly and unreal.

I ran my hands along her hips, squeezing her ass as she spread her thighs wider, giving me access to her body and offering me control.

"He's using you against me," she muttered but I wasn't listening.

"Shhhh...moan for me, Elora. Only for me."

And she did, so very sweetly as I curled my tongue around her clit. Her thighs shook as I coerced her into playing with me. Another forced moan emerged from deep down in her diaphragm and her body moved like a perfect wave, crashing her head back against the wall as her fingers dug into my head, forcing me to drink from her well. She tugged on my hair; the sting of that harsh tug only made my hellhound snarl as it bit down on her clit.

"Beau!"

"Yes. Scream for me sweet girl " I soothed her ache with a sweep of my tongue while her juices dripped from that tempting opening.

I spread her thighs wider, hungrily swallowing every drop of her. Sucking on her puffed up lips, now red from my violent takeover.

In her current state of delirium, she didn't notice as I slid up her body, kissing every inch of her. Nor did she notice how her hips were rotating upward, her pussy aching for something, yet not knowing what.

I lifted her, folding her back over the nearest surface. A leather chair that stood against the window.

I smiled down at her as I leaned back to watch her body arch and sway, begging for my touch. She was needy for me, and I let the lust roll through me this time.

Grabbing her breasts, I pinched the nipples, enjoying the way she whimpered and bit her lip. A deep blush painted her cheeks while she shyly looked away from me. She was a conundrum of elicit responses. One moment she was looking away, the next she was arching her back, her naked form undulating erotically.

Fuck. I could just sit back and watch the beauty of how her body succumbed to the pleasure I offered. It rolled over her in evident waves that drove her hips up, rising and falling so seductively.

She planted the soles of her feet on the arm of the leather chair and began to dance. Her pussy rubbing itself on my hardened cock.

"This is so wrong," she breathed again, and my smile only got darker as she elicited the prettiest moans.

"Feels good, doesn't it? To let go. To breathe life into your loins."

My hellhound rumbled, my claws growing long and sharp as they gently scratched her torso, breaking just enough skin for a slight amount of crimson to seep out.

She arched back, gripping the edge of the seat as my beast devoured her. Leaning forward, my hellhound's tongue lapped at the wounds. The taste of copper filling my mouth and my senses as I couldn't get enough of her.

"Beau, please don't do this to me. Please."

"You say the words, but your body has a mind of its own. Look."

We both stared down at her wet pussy sliding itself all over my cock. It's red mushroomed head looked angry and ready to fuck.

"Please don't," she whispered. Once again attempting a weak shove at my chest.

As I crouched down over her, her pussy slid over the head of my dick.

"Take what you want, and I'll leave," I grunted.

She became frantic in her movements. Her hands clawing at my chest, her hips rotating on my hard length. My cock spurted cream onto her delicate mound, and I groaned, fisting the cushion above her head to keep from moving.

"Take it," I begged her, and she screamed. Clawing her

way down my back as she came for me. I dipped my hips, allowing the pressure to build as we rubbed each other. Her hand suddenly enclosed around the base of my cock, and she stared up at me, lips trembling as she stroked me.

I shut my eyes tight, loving that softness of her. That scent of her pussy engulfing every rational thought I had. My hellhound wanted to hump at her. To just take and take but as a man I let her go at her own pace. We linked eyes, and this heat rolled over me as she jacked me off. I grunted as my hips thrusted against her gentle hands.

"Fuck me," I growled, and she did something I didn't expect.

She pushed back and sat up on her knees. She then took that monster between my legs and put it in her mouth. That delicate tongue of hers, gently lapping at it, encircling the head before it disappeared down her tight throat.

"Arrghhh," I exhaled a low rumble as my cock grew thick and looked mean.

She moaned around it, her eyes on me the entire time as that innocent mouth was sucking my dick. It was fucking glorious. My own personal angel at my mercy.

She ran her tongue along my growing length. The hellhound gave out guttural sounds that weren't human. She moaned around me as my cock grew hard and heavy. Two of her hands worked in unison to tug on it in hard pulls as her mouth sucked out my cream.

I slid my claws into her hair. Holding on as every muscle in my body tensed, I lifted off my toes and I roared as my cock exploded on her tongue.

She was such a good little whore. Lapping up the cream and feeding off the beast.

I fell into the chair, dragging her up easily onto my lap. My cock was still hard between us.

"This can't continue like this," she whispered against my chest as her hand continued to tug on me.

"Mmnnngh," I shifted my hips, giving her access to it. "What if we just give in."

"We can't. It'll destroy us both."

"I don't mind. I'm already destroyed if I can't have you."

My lips found hers as she pressed my dick against her mound. Rubbing herself with it. I reached down between us and fiddled with her clit. She squirmed against me, jerking me off as she panted into my mouth while my fingers rubbed her clit.

"You drive me crazy," she murmured against my lips, and I growled.

I slid two fingers inside of her, my dick held between her thighs. We both looked down, our foreheads pressed together in earnest as we got each other off.

"Right there. Don't stop," she flung her head back, squeezing the tip of my cock.

I gripped the back of the chair, my hips rolling up as her pussy muscles contracted around my fingers.

"Oh my God!"

Those primal sounds of pleasure blended together on my tongue, getting lost against my mouth.

We both held onto each other as our bodies quieted. I was still semi-hard and not fully satisfied but it was sufficient for now.

"I'll only take you if you want me to, Elora."

I pressed my cheek against the top of her head, cuddling her against me. The hellhound purred harshly in my head, and I could tell he was enjoying her hands on us.

"What will happen to me if we can't find my soul?"

"Maybe it's for the best. If I can't find it neither, can he."

"Then what happens to you?"

"The deal was for a million souls. If I can't complete it, I assume I'll serve him for all eternity."

She stayed quiet but I could sense her apprehension.

"I've fought too hard for it to end this way."

She got up and scrambled for her clothes.

"Where are you going?"

"Home. Where I belong. Because clearly I do not belong here."

"The hell you don't!"

I grabbed her elbow and whirled her around to face me. "Tell me you didn't feel something. Tell me I'm still nothing to you."

She was fierce, I'd give her that. "You mean nothing to me."

We stared at each other, knowing damn well that wasn't true.

"Liar."

"Let me go. I want to go home and wash your scent of brimstone off me. It makes me gag."

"Liars go to hell, Elora."

"Maybe that's where I belong after what you've succumbed me to. I can't believe I let this happen."

She whirled on me, taking me off guard. "This shouldn't have happened! It's a sin of the flesh. It's wrong!"

"Don't give me that Bible bullshit! You know damn well it's only wrong when there's no love."

She managed to give out a laugh that dripped with sarcasm. "Love is bullshit!"

Her eyes were fire as she looked at me. "You're going to tell me you love me now? Talk about lies!"

I stood there trying to make sense of how things had escalated so quickly.

"You realize that this is ridiculous!" I shouted after her.

"It's not like all humanity hasn't done this."

She turned to me, rage and fear traced her eyes. "The rest of humanity hasn't had their souls condemned to the devil."

I looked away from her as she continued to fuss around the room searching for her shoe, and when she found it, she waved it in my face.

"This can't happen again."

I grabbed a pair of pants, hopping into them as I followed her to the door. "You think this is easy for me!"

She ran out into the hallway, punching the elevator button as she ignored me.

"Hey! You look at me when I'm talking to you." I swung her around to face me and instantly regretted it as the tears that fell down her cheeks broke me inside.

"Elora," her name now sounded like a far distant star. One that was pretty to look at but could never be reached. And she'd lit up my darkness just like so many stars do.

"Please Beau, just let me go."

"You know I can't do that."

"Then good luck to you, Beau." She stroked my bare chest and the hellhound purred.

"The next time we see each other will be the last time."

The elevator doors opened, and she slid inside, turning to face me.

"Goodbye, Beau."

"I hope you know who you're up against, Elora."

She nodded just as a solitary tear strummed down her cheek.

"My soul."

The doors closed and I clenched my chest as that burning sensation returned, only this time it didn't subside. It was a clear reminder of what I was losing.

Elora

CHAPTER TWENTY-FOUR

White Lies We tell

"You've been fighting sin this entire time. Maybe the way in is by letting him drag you down."

"What the hell are you talking about?"

Karma sighed, feeling as exasperated as I was.

"Think about it. Your mother bound your souls together. If he drags you down, what's to stop the magic from setting you both free when he completes his contract?"

"Impossible. The spell has clearly hidden and trapped our souls. Not even Lucifer can get to them."

"Right. But it's the only way you can find your soul. Ashdemai has corrupted your body, but both your souls are intact."

"Not if I allow Beau to take the one guarantee that I have that I haven't been tainted by evil."

"There are no guarantees, Elora! That's a fucking myth. If not, we'd all be burning in hell by now."

152

"Who's to say we won't?"

I slumped down on the sofa. "My soul isn't mine anymore, Karma. So what the fuck am I fighting for?"

She sighed and sat down beside me, cradling my hands. "Please don't give up."

"I don't want to, but nothing makes sense anymore."

"Babe. Do you love him?"

I stood up, turning away from her. "It doesn't matter."

"Of course, it does! It's not wrong if you love him."

"You don't know that!"

"I know you've blinded yourself to this, but love is powerful. Your mother is a perfect example of that."

"What if I did? It means nothing. Once a soul is promised to him, it's his. I've lost what I'm fighting for."

"Then find something to hold onto."

"Even if I did, what you're saying is a suicide."

"What do you have to lose? The realms exist. We know this. You need to see it for yourself and Beau's your only way in."

"But what if I can't get out?"

"I swear on my own damn soul that I will get you out."

"We'll that's a stupid wager." The male's voice appeared out of nowhere. And we both jumped, startled.

Karma leapt back as Kimaris appeared before us.

"Who is that?" She whispered to me.

"He's a fallen angel."

"Holy shit." She seemed to scream in a hushed tone, her eyes fixed on the brawny half naked demon that stood before us.

"They exist?"

"Yes. But they're not good."

"He definitely looks like an angel," she murmured, biting down on her lip.

"If I were a lesser demon, I would have already taken that wager."

"It's not a wager." She squared off her shoulders, confronting him. I had to admit, my friend had balls. Brass ones.

Kimaris stopped and eyed her for a long time. "You look familiar. Do I know you?"

Karma smirked. "Honey I've seen a lot of you come and go through these doors. Believe me I would remember if I'd met you," she raised a now and placed a hand on her hip as she sized him up.

"And I have to say, I do not remember meeting you."

I interrupted them, before he could continue their conversation.

"I think we have more pressing matters here, don't you? You can flirt with the human later, Kimaris. What are you doing here?"

He blinked twice before responding. "I couldn't help but listen in on what your human friend here..."

"Karma," she stated her name.

He paused and clenched his jaw. She was getting to him and if I wasn't so anxious for answers, I would have laughed. She tended to do that to people. In particular, men. After a moment of hesitation, he continued.

"What *Karma* was saying. It may work."

I looked at him in protest, but he raised his hand to quiet us both down.

"He'll never do it willingly, Elora. The spell your mother initiated made him your protector."

"I know that."

"You have to convince him otherwise."

"You've both gone crazy."

"Maybe. But it's the only way to beat this curse. Beau Kavanaugh has to complete his contract."

"It's impossible. There's no soul to take."

He pressed a finger to his lips. "They don't know that," he said in a low hushed tone.

"What if Lucifer finds out and doesn't set him free?

"Beau risks his freedom no matter what."

"What will happen to both of us?"

"I cannot tell you that because the last time this happened, it all went wrong."

"I don't know about this." I said, shaking my head.

"I can guarantee one thing. If you truly love him and he truly loves you, then you will be together again. His essence will find yours instantly. Wherever his soul is, yours lies. Remember that."

I stared at him, a quiver in my tone. "But what if I don't make it out."

Karma reached for me, draping an arm around my shoulders.

"I promise I'll get you out," she whispered.

I fixed my eye on Kimaris. "I won't risk her."

"You won't have to. I'll be there when you call."

"What about Beau?"

"Beau and I have an agreement. I'm only waiting for him to make his move."

"Will he know?"

"I'll let him know as soon as your heart stops beating."

"How can I trust you?"

"You can't. But I've been promised payment in the form of a hellhound."

"Beau's hellhound?"

He nodded and the thought was bittersweet. I was growing fond of his hound.

"I'm so confused." I slid down into the comforts of my couch. Karma sat beside me.

"I bet you he is too. He needs to see that it's the only way."

I looked up at Kimaris. "You're basically saying I'll be the bait."

"That's exactly what I'm saying."

"Beau isn't going to like this."

"That's why he can't find out until the last minute."

"He can smell the lies on me."

"Then make sure you believe them too."

My heart was in my throat, but I had been training for this moment my entire life. I had to defend what was mine and both my soul and Beau's were now mine to fight for.

I nodded and straightening my shoulders I stood before Kimaris.

"If you let me down, I will hunt you down and torture your sorry ass for all eternity."

He smirked. "You two do belong together."

I turned to Karma. "Don't get in the way."

"But..."

I shook my head firmly. "I'll never forgive you if you do. Live, Karma. Do it for me. I need you to live."

"I love you."

She pulled me into a tight hug, and I stayed there in that warmth for a long time before finally pulling away.

My decision was made, and I was ready to do this, no matter how scared I really was.

Beau

CHAPTER TWENTY-FIVE

A Little Death

The knock on the door gave me pause, but I already knew who stood on the other side of it. I opened it, leaning on the doorframe.

"You're back."

"I am." She pushed past me, and I was forced to let her in.

I followed her into the living room where she whirled around and fixed those pretty brown eyes on me.

"I need you to take me to purgatory."

"What the hell are you talking about?"

The hellhound sniffed the air, and I took a step toward her, bringing us close enough that our bodies touched.

She's up to something.

"Yes, she is." I murmured.

I don't like it.

"Me neither."

She stood there, with her hands on her hips, just watching me.

"What is it, Elora?"

"I'm just waiting for you two to be done."

She began to pace, looking like a tiger wanting out of her cage, and my hellhound liked the view.

She kept folding and unfolding her hands as she continued to walk back and forth along the length of the small apartment.

"He told me to lie, I can't lie to you."

"Who told you to lie?"

"Kimaris. He said you'd never let me go."

"He's right."

"He said you accepted his help."

I nodded. "He offered it."

"Did you know?"

"Did I know what?" I whispered, playing with a tendril of her hair.

"Did you know about my mother?"

I sighed, turning away from her and propping my hands on my knees.

"I know she put a spell on my hellhound. Turned him into some sort of demon protector. How fucking absurd."

"Is that all you know?"

I avoided her eyes, not wanting to admit I knew what we were.

"Beau?" She cradled my cheek, turning my head to face her.

"I can't do ss you ask. I don't have it in me." I looked down at my shaking hands and jerked when her hand slid over my sigil.

"You can't, but he can."

The hellhound felt anxious, cause he also knew that what she was asking was dangerous.

"Just do it."

She looked up at me and I knew what she was about to do. She was a complete suicide mission.

Slowly she shrugged off her leather jacket. Underneath it she wore a tight silk dress, the hem of the skirt ended at her calves. She was encased in black lace, and it molded to all those curves, pulling her tots together, wrapping itself around her soft belly and hugging the wide expanse of her hips. I swallowed hard, my hands tightening into fists at my side, holding myself back from touching her. The sight of her sent a thrill to my cock and the hellhound trembled.

"Do your worst," I muttered, and her eyes told me everything.

They grew dark, sultry, and she was taking on the challenge I'd presented her.

What do we do?

The hellhound began to move, his need matching my own. I was more in control than he was.

Let me out. It salivated.

"Now is not the time."

Either you take her or I will. The hellhound snarled and I felt it wanting to force its way through.

My walls came up and the chains locked on the cage I kept him in. His anger rolled through me, and I kept myself calm while I continued to watch her.

I was caught between doing the right thing and making her mine. Yet I was paralyzed, curious to see what she would do next. She didn't disappoint.

Running her hands up behind her, she slid the zipper of the dress down, when it pooled at her feet, my dick responded.

She stood there, her tots out and edible, her pussy covered in a sheer panty that outlined those sweet lips.

My cock grew hard, and she knew exactly what she was

doing to me. At that moment, I didn't know how to react. If I dragged her down to hell, I'd never see her again. If I let her go, I'd be condemned to hell for all eternity. Either way, she wasn't going to give me a choice.

Those eyes of hers fixed on me as she moved across the room. I saw the reflection of myself in the mirror across from us. My legs were in a wide stance, fists at my sides, tension ran through the muscles of my bare arms. The sigil on my chest was pulsing a deep red and my eyes had that same gold hue that only she ignited.

Her feminine form filled the reflection. I tightened my jaw as her scent engulfed us. She was just as needy as we were.

Let me out.

The hellhound rattled the bars of that cage, its desperation flowing through me. But when she got down on her knees before me, running those damn hands over my hardened dick, I knew something bad was about to happen, and all I could do was brace myself.

Her eyes never left mine as she undid my slacks. Nor did she look away as she took out the monster between my legs. It was thick and heavy, and ready for her.

The hellhound shivered as she dragged her nails over it, teasing us as she placed the head of it in her mouth, biting down on it lightly, dragging those teeth over it. I hissed and she smiled at me, so fucking wickedly, that the hound growled in that arcane guttural way that vibrated down to my toes.

Her eyes locked on me, keeping me in a seductive trance, just as I watched her mouth close over me. I staggered back from the pleasure, the hellhound rattling the cage as she sucked us to the back of her throat, her teeth rolled over the edge of my head and that was our undoing.

I roared as the hellhound tore through me. Its claws tore through my fingertips, long and sharp as they kept her head on our cock.

Her eyes widened as my dick thickened against her tongue. I screamed as the hellhound morphed enough to feel her suction.

My hair grew out, my body grew hairier, my shoulders broader, my eyes glowed red like the flames from the depths of hell below.

I cried out as my bones cracked just enough to give me my hound-like frame. He didn't shift completely, punishing me for keeping him away. Instead, he kept me suspended in that agony as Elora continued her torture on us both.

She dug her nails in us, as the demon in me fucked her mouth. It groaned and purred in its arcane way as it drove our body into her.

We gripped her hair tight, positioning her head down so we could slide in deeper. She gagged over and over, spit dangling from her lips as she took a ragged breath, looking all the sexier as we rubbed our cock on her lips and she ate it up, a hungry moan reverberating along the base.

"Fuck," we both groaned angrily as he shoved her back, pouncing over her.

"Do it," she urged us and the hellhound responded the best way he knew how.

Leaning forward, his snout breathed in her scent, and opening his mouth, he gripped her neck.

"Don't!" I begged him, as the taste of copper filled our tongue.

She's ours.

I knew what he was doing. He was making me see this was something I couldn't stop. He gently lay her down onto the floor and her soft caress soothed the hellhound. She petted him like the frail dog he was and he let her, nuzzling at her neck and allowing her to subdue the demon.

I reached out for her comfort, and she gave it to me freely as the hellhound allowed me to shift back.

Her hands cradled my face when she saw me, and she gave me a sad smile.

"I'm done fighting, Beau. Just take me to him."

I shook my head. "I can't do that."

"Yes, you can."

"I won't do that."

"You have to, Beau."

"No, I don't."

"We have to end this."

"I won't do it like this. I won't give him the satisfaction."

"Beau," she turned my face, forcing me to look at her.

"You have to let me go."

"I can't," I said in earnest, pressing my forehead to hers as I slumped into her arms.

I held onto her, afraid to let her go. Afraid that if I did, another would come and tear her to pieces right before destroying me.

I was hard for her, needy, and being in her arms wasn't helping the situation. It the worst form of torture you could ever imagine.

I pulled back, staring down at her pretty face. "Why didn't you trust me enough to include me in your wicked plans?"

"Because I don't trust anyone. Least of all a demon."

"Fair enough," I uttered. "But now what?"

"Now we give into what he wants."

"He wants you."

She nodded and smiled. "Then maybe it's time I became his."

"What are you doing?"

"Just follow my lead," she whispered and kissed my neck. "If I'm bound to you, and you're set free..."

"This is a dangerous game you're playing, Elora."

"So play with me. We both have nothing to lose."

She drew me down over her and my muscles flexed from that electrical current she had on me when her body arched and writhed against mine.

"I have everything to lose. Your soul is bound to mine, Elora. It's true. That witch of a mother of yours, knew exactly how to protect you and ruin me in the process. I'm meant to protect you. It's the only thing I know that is real in my entire existence."

"Then let me fight for the one thing we both want," temptation whispered.

"A soul for a sin. That will condemn us both."

Angst shone in her eyes as she caressed my face and then slowly, she tugged me down to her.

Our lips met, hers gently brushing mine. "See, i told you, you weren't such a bad guy."

"You're turning me into one," I growled.

"Take me. If I'm yours he can't have me."

"He'll always have you."

She shook her head. "Not in my heart he won't."

Reaching up, she caressed my face, looking at me with this look that spoke of love...for me. It was a look I didn't think I'd ever get to see.

"I love you," I murmured against her lips.

She pressed her fingertips to my lips. "Hush. You can't love me, Beau. Saying that can get us both in trouble."

"But I do love you. I'd do anything for you."

"You have no idea what you're saying, Beau."

"I'm saying, I love you. I'm saying I'd give my soul for yours."

The hellhound howled in my head. The pain I held so close to my chest, slowly engulfed me.

"It's not your soul to give anymore, Beau. It's his. Just like I am his."

"You're mine," the demon in me rose to the occasion. "No one can have you but me."

"That's right," she urged, and I fell for it.

"Do it. Take me to him."

"You'll always be mine."

"It's the only way, Beau. I need you to do this for me."

I hesitated. And as she reached up to cradle my cheek. I kissed the inside of her palm.

"Love is so strange, isn't it?" She murmured.

"How is that?"

"Because who would have thought I'd come to love the one thing I've hated most in my entire life."

Her words made me tense up. My cock perched at her entrance. Our eyes met and she smiled, urging me with a slight nod. I didn't think. I simply gave her what she asked for. Fuck. I'd give her the world if I could.

Her sweet cry of release echoed around us as I filled her with every inch of me. She scrambled back, partially fighting me as her nails scratched the floorboards beneath her. I pinned her down with my hips as I watched that beautiful pain tear through her. One swift thrust and I had plunged through her barrier and was now buried deep inside of her. I stilled. Holding both myself and the hellhound back. My animal instinct heightened by his.

This one action had condemned us both to hell and yet I knew, taking her would mean that Lucifer couldn't have that one part of her. Her innocence belonged to me.

She gasped as I pulled out and slammed back into her. My name, now a plea on her lips.

"Beau."

Her kind eyes watched me, and she knew I was struggling. The turmoil shone in the red embers that lit up my pupils.

She shifted slightly and moaned quietly from that sweet pain. It made my cock pulse and grow thicker inside of her, my hellhound emerging in my need.

"Beau."

My name fell from her lips as her hands played with my hair and then two words ignited my lust for her.

"Fuck me."

Her wish was my fucking command, and I did as she asked of me. I fucked her deep and hard. Filling her with every inch of me, unable to satiate this need for her. I'd condemned us both, the moment my cock slid into her tight cunt. Her cry of pleasure was our defeat. She'd fallen victim to my impure cravings. Those carnal persuasions that were going to ruin us both.

I growled while my hellhound shifted slightly, my cock thickening inside of her. Those innocent eyes went wide, and she strained against me as the demon inside of me fed off her pleasure. A succubus that enjoyed her sobs as it sullied her innocence - reveling in defiling her beautiful body.

My hellhound shook, rumbling as I held it at bay. I couldn't let it shift while I was buried inside of her. I was sure it would traumatize her, and she'd had enough pain as it was.

"You're stretching me," she whined.

"Does it feel good?" I nipped at her neck, allowing my hands to cup her breasts.

"Yes. God, yes."

"I'm not a god, Elora. I'm your demon."

I sucked on her nipple, gaining a long purring moan from her.

"Yes, I know what you are."

"Then say my name, Elora. Say it loud enough for your dark prince to hear."

I slid myself in deeper, fucking her in long torturous strokes.

"Beau."

"Louder." I grunted, the head of my cock swelling.

"Beau!" My name was a loud, pleasure filled moan and my cock expanded, pulsing inside of her.

Instinctively. I knew what was happening. Elora's body tensed, arching back in my arms. I knew this was too much for her to take for her first time, but my hound wouldn't let her get away with not taking every bit of his cock, and that included the knot.

Before it inflated to its full girth, I slammed into her, letting it grow inside her, her screams of climax bouncing off the walls as he locked us together. The tip of my cock pulsing while her pussy held it in a pounding grip that massaged along its heavy length.

I wouldn't dare pull out, not until it was all done, thrusting shortly and sharply, I made it as pleasurable for her as I possibly could.

The hellhound snarled viciously, eyes ablaze with lust, though thrust after thrust had his head spinning, wanting more, growling deep in the back of his throat. To breed, to fuck... He didn't care, I couldn't care, snarling and slamming in, chest juddering with every snatched breath.

Her orgasm came swiftly as her pussy gripped my dick in climax. I was hardly able to move, driving in short, sharp thrusts as the locking influence of my demon's knot took us over.

Elora screamed my name, clawing at my back in a desperate attempt to push me away.

"Fuuuck..." she groaned, falling limp in my arms.

I growled, nuzzling her soft breasts, and sliding her nipples between my growing fangs.

"I can't," she shuddered as small orgasms fluttered through her.

"Can't what, my love?"

"I can't take anymore," she breathed. Her body trembling as the knot that held us continued to give her pleasure.

"You're mine," that rumble came from deep within my chest as she clung to me.

"You were meant for me," she whispered in my ear, and I strained against her. My groin rubbed against her as the hellhound bellowed out a low howl.

"Beau."

"Mine," it snarled as my body stretched out. I cried out as pain ricocheted down to my groin and my cock exploded just as I shifted above her.

I slipped an arm around her as she tried to disengage, but her pussy kept milking my cock.

"It'll be a while before that softens..." I grunted, cum still spurting, fighting through gasps of breath to get my words out. "And not a drop is going to leak out."

The knot was bulbous and pressed on her G-spot as she climaxed again and again, helpless in my arms. The knot locked us together, forced there by my dick. My body echoed her moan as we trembled in delight.

The hellhound had managed to have its way with us, slightly emerging from its cage. It whimpered and nuzzled at her neck as it rutted into her with incessant strokes.

Her soft groans filled my ears as she stroked my ears and head.

She let him fuck her in those last few seconds before we all tired out, collapsing into each other. I thought tasting her was enough of a reminder of what life had felt like, but I was wrong. Being buried deep inside of her was a religious experience all on its own.

"What was that?"

I shook my head. "The hellhound. It took over."

"I felt it swell. I didn't know..."

"I didn't want to scare you."

"You didn't scare me, Beau. I knew you were there the entire time."

"But he fucked you too. He took what he wanted."

She smiled and reached up to touch my cheek. "He's a part of you, isn't he?"

I turned away from her. "Sadly, yes."

"Did you feel it?"

I looked back into her soul bearing eyes. "To my very core."

She smiled. "Me too."

I leaned over her and kissed her. A soft kiss. One that came purely from me. The hellhound growled in my head, but I ignored him as I took my small piece of her.

Her sweetness.

"What happens now?" She whispered.

"It's either me or someone else, Elora."

"I'm sure we'll meet again someday."

Her words caught me off guard. "Maybe."

I brushed her hair away from her face and kissed her forehead.

"Ready?"

"As ready as I'll ever be," she murmured slowly, closing her eyes.

"We're bound forever, sweets. I'll find you. Wherever you're hiding, I will find you." I whispered into her ear. Holding her tight.

And for the first time in years, I looked up to the heavens and I prayed. But I didn't pray for my soul. No. I prayed for hers. Because if there was one thing in this existence that didn't deserve any pain, it was my Elora.

Beau

Death's Veil

he's dead.

S The hellhound's sorrow lay over us like a dark cloak. I crouched over her sleeping, knowing she was gone.

"Elora?" I whispered her name, shaking her lightly as I watched her eyelids flutter.

She's not dead.

Relief flooded over us. "No. Worse. She's dreaming."

Neither of us knew what would happen if I took her. I expected to take down her spirit. I expected screams and pain, but this was something else entirely. Something else was at work here and I had a feeling I knew exactly who held all the answers.

Within seconds I was slamming through the doors of her quaint little store. I'd paid enough attention to Elora to know that she kept everything in this location, especially her mother's books. What I didn't expect to find was the redhead behind the counter.

"You must be the hellhound." She shut the book she had her head in and fixed her big green eyes on me.

"And you must be the witch."

She spread her arms and gave me a tight smile. "The one and only." She tilted her head to give me a once over. "I thought you'd be...bigger."

I smirked. "My hellhound would disagree."

"Hmmm, it would appear so."

"I need your help."

"Is it Elora?" Her tone changed instantly to that of a scared child's.

"Is she alright? Did she..."

"She's.... not herself right now."

"Is she dead? Did your hellhound finally take her?"

"No."

"Then what is it?"

"I don't know where she is."

"But you were with her, right? You were supposed to be with her!"

"Well, we were *supposed* to be a lot of things, but instead we're stuck in this godless limbo."

The witch looked concerned, and I followed close as she made her way toward the back of the store.

"This is not how things were supposed to go." She cleared the table setting a black and white candle in the center. She slammed down a book, Flipping through the pages.

"And how were they supposed to go..." I stopped, not knowing her name.

"Karma. My name is Karma. And you were not supposed to leave her side.

"She didn't leave much choice in the matter."

"Damn, stubborn girl."

"What are you looking for?"

I could see her mind spinning as she scanned the small store. Grabbing a gold thread, she wrapped it around each candle then handed me a lighter.

"Light the damn candles."

"What for?"

"To conjure a goddamn fallen angel."

"And the thread?"

"To restrain the mother fuckers.

I smirked. "I knew I'd like you."

She smiled. "That I can do."

I call upon the angels
Light and Dark
May the one named Kimaris
Be found in the fog
Dark angel, lend me thy light,
And through death's veil wander into my sight.

Thunder cracked and a swift breeze swept through, cutting out the candlelight. In the blink of an eye I heard what sounded like a grunt and in the middle of the floor, kept in a secure witch's circle, lay Kimaris. Chained and passed off.

"What's the meaning of this?" He held his bound wrists up into the light and Karma rounded the table to face him.

"You lied to us."

"I did no such thing."

"Then where is Elora!"

"She's supposed to be with him." He gestured at me, and both sets of eyes fixed on me.

"What games are you playing at, Kimaris?"

"I'm not playing any games. She went to you because you were the only one to bring her down."

Anger flooded through my veins and the hellhound reared back, ready for a fight.

"You damn well know that I was unable to do that. Now she's lying on my bed, in a fucking coma."

"So she's alive?"

"Did you expect there to be casualties?"

"Actually. I expected her to be ripped apart. This situation is unprecedented but intriguing."

"She's not a fucking science experiment."

"No. But she is uncanny. Something our realm has never heard of."

"Why did you do it Kimaris?"

"Both of you needed a nudge. The more you wait, the more Lucifer grows impatient. If he grows suspicious, we'll have no window of time."

"You were sent by him, weren't you?"

"I work for myself. I already told you that. You're clouded by sentiment and anger. Careful hellhound, you leap over, and you'll be face to face with Wrath."

"She's not a stranger in my world," I snarled.

Karma gestured for me to step away from the circle and with a quick flick of her wrist, she threw holy water in his face.

The blessed water sizzled on his flesh. "Fuuuck!"

I smirked. "Seems like having a witch in your corner can be beneficial."

"There's only so much insult I will endure, human."

Karma smiled. "I have to admit, you're kinda sexy when you're pissed off."

"Where is Elora, Kimaris?"

"You said she was dreaming. She dreams a lot, doesn't she?"

It took me a second to realize what he was saying. I reached out, grabbing Karma's wrist before she announced him again.

"Wait."

"He knows where she is. He promised me he'd keep her safe." Her eyes landed on his and he bowed his head.

"Her subconscious is lost in purgatory."

"Ashdemai's doing."

"Most likely."

"Son of a bitch," I murmured.

"But she's alive, right? Karma tugged on my sleeve.

"Yes, for now. Which makes her vulnerable."

I looked down at Kimaris. "How do I get her back?"

"You can start by having your witch release me. I'm the only one who can go to her. I can't hear her if you keep me chained here. I'm no good to her like this."

Karma moved to release him, but I placed my hands over hers.

"You already went behind my back; how do I know you have no other motives?"

"My only motive lies in the fate of your hound. I'm not against you, Beau. But time is running out."

I paused, thinking things through but still making sense of nothing. I let go if Karma and she leaned forward, whispering an incantation and releasing the monster.

He instantly lunged for her, lifting and slamming her down on the table. His hand wrapped around her neck as he pinned her down.

"You went too far, witch."

"If you don't return her to me, you'll see how far I can go."

He released her, stunned by her response. She didn't cower and he seemed taken aback by that. She reminded me of Elora, strong willed and a fighter till the end.

"What's the plan, Kimaris?"

He continued to look down at Karma as he spoke. "I'll go rescue your human. But you'll need to go see Lucifer. Bide us as much time as you can."

"And how much time is that?"

He tore his eyes away from the witch and turned to me.

"As much as it takes for her to release your damned soul."

I didn't want to trust him, but something in my gut told me this fallen angel, this defector, was our only hope.

"You better not fuck this up, angel."

Karma slowly sat up and glanced at her before responding.

"Why would I? I've been promised a hellhound. And that is not something I'll give up easily."

"I hope not," I uttered.

Karma glanced at me, and I closed my eyes and bowed my head slightly, reassuring her that I'd get Elora back. Even if it's the last thing I did in this world, I'd get her back.

Elora

CHAPTER TWENTY-SEVEN

Blessed Souls

Hell's Gates weren't quite how I'd pictured them. An endless barren land, cold and desolate. A long, drawn-out line lay ahead as convicts, murderers, liars and sinners awaited their penance. Waiting on line to get into Hell felt as if you were waiting for an execution. Everyone seemed sickly, riddled with insecurities as every possible source of anxiety and doubt were whispered in your ear. They made it the most unpleasant of experiences.

I don't know how long I'd been standing there, since time was irrelevant here. I wish Kimaris would have told me this. I also wished he would have mentioned the gushes of wind and rivers of blood that were prominent in this, what they called a realm. But I knew this couldn't be hell nor could it be the heaven humanity raved about.

Neither Beau nor his hound were with me. I was where I dreaded most, and I was alone.

Kimaris.

I called out to the angel, hoping he'd hear me, but hours passed and he was nowhere in sight.

"Kimaris!" I yelled out.

The souls barely looked at me, as they continued on their own paths. Through the lightning that cracked between the gray clouds up above, the sound of flapping wings thundered overhead. The shadow of those wings appeared first before Kimaris' form landed on one knee before me.

"Is that your usual entrance?"

"I enjoy it," he shrugged.

"Where were you?"

"I was being held up?"

"By what?"

"A witch, a hellhound, and your boyfriend."

"Oh no," I pressed a hand to my lips.

"Don't worry. I think we're all on the same page from this point on. At least I hope so."

"Didn't think fallen angels had hope."

"I fell to walk among your own. I never lost hope, Elora."

I took a long look at him and realized Kimaris had his own suffering, and it was deep and painful. Maybe one day I'd ask him about it. Right now, I had my own suffering to deal with.

"What is this place?"

"I'd say it was the line into hell but it's where souls wait to be condemned."

"Why am I here and not with Beau?"

"Your body is still alive. The hellhound is watching over it."

"I don't understand."

"You have no soul, just your essence...your subconscious."

"My mind is trapped here."

He looked apprehensive in his response. "Yes."

I grabbed his arm and his wavering gaze finally landed on me.

"They told me you've been having dreams."

"You knew about Ashdemai?

"Not entirely."

"Where is Beau?"

"Let's just say he's biding us some time."

"Until what, exactly?"

"Until you free him."

He turned away and I grabbed his arm. "Hey! I need you to tell me step by step what is going on here, or I will not move from this spot."

Kimaris bowed his head and smiled. "She told me you'd be stubborn."

"Who? Who told you?"

"Your mother."

I froze. "You knew my mother?"

"Your mother was a powerful witch. One who helped a lot of people along the way. She helped me once, gave me guidance when I was lost, and I promised to return the favor."

"Is she here?"

He shook his head. "She's on a level I haven't been able to reach in a long time."

"Is she at peace?"

"I can't answer that, Elora."

"Did she ask you to help me?"

"Not exactly. Unfortunately, I wasn't able to get to her in time. But I knew she cared for you, and I had heard of Beau's dealings throughout the years."

"So you're truly helping me."

"I'll take you where you need to go. Payment has already been made."

"And what happens to you after we're done?"

He looked out into that desolate abyss. "I finally get to seek my vengeance."

I hesitated, thinking back on everything that had happened. Why this angel wanted to help me, I didn't understand. But I needed all the help I could get.

"Where did they say this cage was hidden?"

"It's not easy to get to. Lucifer has it well protected."

"All I have to do is release, Beau. He goes free and I go with him. You had me come here for a reason. If you want to help me, be my guide."

His mouth was drawn in a tight grim line. "We'll have to walk for a while. But Elora, I have to insist here that you become aware that there are no guarantees."

"If I release him, Lucifer has nothing to wage, and I have nothing to lose."

I couldn't imagine spending eternity in a place like this. I shivered from the constant windstorm that encircled us, carrying within it the agonized whispers of the dead. It only increased my anxiety.

Kimaris turned to me before heading up what treacherous path.

"When I tell you to close your eyes, you close them."

"Why?"

"Just do as I say. And no matter what happens, don't ever look them in the eye."

"What?"

He was done talking, turning his back to me, he started up the path. I gasped at the sight of human faces that were buried in the ground. Their limbs shook as they extended their bony hands toward me. I ran up behind

Kimaris and he turned his head slightly, giving them a quick glance.

"Don't worry about them. They can't get to you. The tars of purgatory have swallowed them up."

"Do they hurt?"

"We all hurt down here, Elora."

We continued on our way. And the higher we went, the colder it became. It wasn't until we were halfway there that Kimaris took his weapon out. I felt helpless, without having anything to protect me.

"Remember what I said."

"Close my eyes, I got it."

He whirled around. Grabbing my jacket and shoving me against the wall. I stared up at him in shock.

"What the fuck!"

"This is not something to take lightly. Do not dare look them in the eyes. If you do, it's over."

"Okay, I heard you."

"No matter what you hear, you keep them closed."

"Okay!"

I shoved his hands off me and we continued our path.

A demonic screeching came from the horizon. Kimaris stopped, his weapon in hand.

"Stand behind me."

The screeching got closer. "What is that?"

"The Fiends."

I glanced up at the sky as black wallowing spirits filled the air.

"Close your eyes!"

I shielded my face from the heathens, crouching low as in the distance I heard Kimaris struggle to fight them.

I could feel them hovering over me, their hissing whispers telling me to look at them. I ignored everyone, falling against the wall as cold hands touched me.

Suddenly, I heard a roar. And within seconds, the spirits were swept off me. Kimaris grabbed me by the hand and hauled me up. When I opened my eyes, the skies were completely black, and Kimaris, bruised and battered, was looking at me.

"Run!"

My eyes widened and my body reacted, breaking out into a run up that mountain. I didn't know where I was going or what I'd find at the top of it, but I could feel the hands of the devil reaching for me as I fled.

Beau

CHAPTER TWENTY-EIGHT

A Broken Contract

I waited for an audience with Lucifer. Not an easy feat, but since I was so well known around these parts, I didn't have a problem getting in.

I left the hellhound protecting Elora. As soon as her soul was back, I had no doubt there would be another trying to snatch her back into hell.

"Have you come to bring me my soul?"

He floated down from above. Black wings spanned behind him. Yet his face remained in the shadows. All he'd let you see were those two glowing eyes that pierced through you as he fixed them on you. I wondered why his face always remained hidden.

Was it shame?

Was it hideous?

Or did he just not want us mere mortals to know just how beautiful he once was.

"Elora Wolfsbane is waiting in purgatory as asked."

Lucifer opened his arms and shut his eyes. Leaning his head back, he listened as the whispers hovered around us. When his eyes shot open, I knew I was in trouble.

"It shouldn't surprise me that the world is full of liars, but it does surprise me when one of my own dares to spit out a falsity."

"It's not a lie. She's down there."

"And her soul?"

"Is lost."

He laughed. "We don't lose souls, nor do they run from us. Were you that weak, Hellhound, that you could not produce such a simple soul."

"I am not weak."

"No, you're just stupid and simple minded. A witch and her daughter got the best of you."

"You knee?"

"I'm disappointed in you, Kavanaugh." His form was suddenly in front of me, and I was forced down to my knees. His face moved like a blur as those eyes glared down at me.

"I expected more from you."

I struggled against the invisible shackles that now restrained me.

"You set me up for failure!"

"All you had to do was find the soul, not play with it. And you and that hellhound did play with it, didn't you?"

I bit my tongue, knowing better than to curse at the devil for I might get my bit off.

"I'm sure Ashdemai had a field day with both of you."

"Ashdemai can burn in the deepest pits of hell."

"Oh, I'm sure he is. Probably enjoying it too, that damn sadomasochist."

"You'll never find her soul."

He clucked his tongue, and one of those gnarly, bony frail fingers with a long-yellowed claw, reached out to trace my cheek. I tried to pull away, but his laughter stopped me.

Lucifer had known all along that I would never get him what he wanted. He knew all along that I'd never complete the contract.

"Never say never."

He knew. He always knew.

"You and your hellhound still have a debt. One you didn't complete."

I looked at either side of my widespread hands, where the burnt souls were coming out, their calloused hands tugging at me.

I looked up at the skies, screaming for Elora. It wouldn't take long for these souls to rip my body, this vessel, apart.

"Did you honestly think I'd release you, when your pet is so close."

My eyes went wide in stunned silence. He pressed his hand over the sigil, and I screamed in agony.

"Ashes to ashes," the bottom part of his face came into view and his smile was as evil and malevolent as he was.

"I'm sure you'll both enjoy each other's company...in the depths of hell."

"No. No!" I shouted.

ELORA

I shook where I stood, knowing this was the end of the line. Kimaris yelled from behind to hurry the hell up, as if my task were that easy.

Everything in my life had led me to this point. The fates had played enough games with us and now here I stood, ready to end them all.

The cage was not metaphoric in the least bit. The cage was a literal golden cage and within it was a small wooden box. What I searched for was inside that ornate box.

"So simple," I muttered as I reached out, scalding my hand as I tried to release the cage.

"Do it now!" Kimaris yelled at me, wielding his sword toward yet another dark spirit.

The fiends swirled around the outer rims of the mountain, unable to get in as much as I was unable to get out.

As I stood there, I could suddenly feel my body grow weak and numb. I fell to my knees as the impact of Beau's pain stunned me.

I could feel him. And not just in my head but around me. His presence was undeniable.

"What are you waiting for?" Kimaris insisted, turning to watch me over his shoulder.

"Something is wrong!"

I closed my eyes, taking a deep breath and in the recesses of my mind I heard.

"Elora!"

"Beau?"

"Elora. I'm here."

"Beau, what's wrong."

"He knows you're bound to me."

"What do I do?"

"Open the cage. It's the only way."

"If I do this, will I ever see you again."

I clenched my eyes tightly, shedding tears that were long past due.

"I'll find you, sweets. I love you, remember."

I nodded. "And I love you."

"Do it."

I reached out, my fingers undoing the lock. There was a flicker of fire, and then suddenly the entire realm dimmed. A gust of wind swirled around me, and I took a deep breath right before that eternal darkness engulfed me.

BEAU

"Please, I beg you. Take my soul for hers."

We needed more time.

"Hmph, such a hero. But heroes are just arrogance and Wrath all wrapped into one."

"Let me go. I'll find you another soul."

"And where's the fun in that?"

I dropped to my knees and pleaded. "Take me and let her go. You can do anything you want with me, just let her go."

"Anything, you say?"

"Yes! Anything!"

"Is that what you truly desire?"

"More than anything in this world."

I shuddered as he smiled. "So be it."

I screamed as I was pulled back with such a force it struck me square in the chest as my spirit was sent back against the wall of blessed souls. Desperate, I tried to struggle free as they reached out to rip at me. All while the devil fixed his enraged eyes on me.

"You dared to fool me. Dared to think you could give me orders!"

His voice shook the ground we stood on. I was dropped

to my knees, and he came at me, a strangled cry of rage was ripped out of him.

And just before he reached me, I was being lifted.

"No! He's mine!!!"

The devil lunged for me, scrambling to grab at me. His claws dug into my legs, ripping at the bone, and I screamed, unable to fight.

Terrifying.

That's the only word I could describe was happening around me. The devil was trying to drag me down while above me there was this golden warmth, I was desperate to reach.

She'd done it. She'd released us. But unfortunately, the devil always had a way.

He yanked me down, enough so he could whisper in my ear.

"We'll meet again soon, Hellhound."

I was floating into the infinite abyss and there was no one there to save me.

Beau

EPILOGUE

An Ever After

T *hree years later...*

I could fill you with lies and tell you we won, but that wouldn't be fair. Because in truth, we all lost something back then.

Elora had released me from that cage and in doing so she had started a turn of events that sent even the fates spinning. Lucifer didn't just let me go. He twisted everything around, reincarnating me, only so that I could find my way to him again.

I'll never forget his words.

You'll come crawling back to me. We'll meet again.

I thought I died at first, but instead it was life's oppression I was feeling. I'd woken up, back at that apartment, drenched in sweat.

It took me a few minutes to realize I no longer had the hellhound in me. And I could feel things like the heat and the cold, and I was thirsty.

The first place I could think of going was to Hell's Doorway. Acheron had quickly taken me in, allowing me to stay as long as I needed. But with all good doorways to hell, this one came with an offer to drown my sorrows in alcohol.

Beau Kavanaugh had a new existence in this world, and I didn't know how to handle it. Elora had forgotten me and everything we were. In turn, I was burdened with remembering everything. The screams, the demons, the hellhound... *her*. I'd say it was a punishment but maybe it was a lesson.

The hellhound had come to me in a dream once. He too had suffered at her loss, but he was grateful, promising he'd always watch over her. He'd gone to Kimaris as promised and he'd thanked me for his freedom. One that wasn't mine to give. It was an odd exchange, as if a part of me was taken from me. Knowing what the devil held in store for me, I imagined we'd be together again one day.

After that, I struggled with hiding from her. And the struggle had become something darker in the last few years. Something more obsessive. Living without her had become hell on earth.

While she bloomed in life and beauty, I sunk in madness and depression. Seeking my solace in alcohol.

I swore I'd never go near her again, but who was I kidding. The Fates had already sealed our fate and in truth my life was nothing without her.

It started out innocent at first. Just watching her, protecting her, but as the years passed, she became my everything. She was the same yet with one significant difference.

She was happy.

It tormented me, that happiness. Because I didn't want to ruin it, but I had my own selfish needs.

I wasn't supposed to find her. I told myself I'd leave her be, but in the end, I couldn't.

I have my flaws and if it came down to it, I was already condemned. She was mine and I was hers. I just needed to remind her of it.

She didn't know I crept into her room late at night. Touching her, scenting her, memorizing every inch of her.

I knew she was lonely and that hole in our hearts was due to the fact that we weren't together.

Tell her....

That voice was in my head, and I shook it away, knowing Ashdemai was not far from it. But he did have a point. I could let her make her own decision.

Take her...

That demon in my head would never let me be.

There's nothing wrong with getting a taste.

I let the voice consume me as I sat there, preying on what once was mine.

She lay quietly, spread out in bed in just her panties and tank top. I liked the sound of her even breaths filling the silence. She had no worries, had no fears. But I was about to change that for her. I needed her. I couldn't live like this anymore. You can call me selfish, you can call me a monster, but I was *her* monster.

I crawled into the bed, hovering over her, remembering every crevice of her. I couldn't help it, she was mine, and I was hers. I was tired of fighting, I just wanted to sink into her and chase my own happiness at her side.

I didn't know if I was going to frighten her, or if she'd fight me. But the monster inside me wanted her to fight. It wanted to rip at her, taste her, make her see I was the only one.

I leaned in, gently dropping a kiss on her lips before I began my descent on her body. She didn't remember me or what I'd taken as mine. So, for her, this would be as if it were that first time.

"I'm your one," I murmured into her ear, as I slid the silky material of her nightgown up and over her breasts.

I groaned, cupping them and rolling the delicate pebbles in between my fingers until she moaned. A slight frown appeared on her forehead, and I vowed to take it away.

I lay beside her, nuzzling her neck as my fingers traced the waistband of her panties. I slid my hand through, finding that soft satin velvety skin between her legs.

I watched her as my fingers found what they were searching for, and I began to slowly circle that hardening bud. I dipped into her juices, swirling them on her clit as she began to grind on me.

"Wake up, baby."

Her eyelids fluttered and I leaned down to take a hard pull on her breast. With my hand locked between her legs, her eyes flew open and one breathless word flew out of her mouth.

"Beau."

Our eyes fixed and we both froze. Her eyes widened and in them I saw the terror, followed by a need so deep it shook me, and then I saw the recognition.

She reached up, cupping my jaw tenderly.

"Are you real?"

I nodded. "I'm real."

"Are you alive?"

I gave out a short laugh. "I'm alive."

"You were in my dreams," she whispered.

"Not anymore," I growled as I bent down and kissed her.

Every desire I'd been hiding was in that kiss. It was hot and needy. Our tongues met in a seductive dance that pulled us together.

"Beau " she broke the kiss; tears fell down her cheeks as my name fluttered from her lips while I continued my assault on her body.

Hearing her say my name again only urged me to take my fill of her. I bit down on her nipple, dragging my teeth along the peak before doing the same to the other.

My hands were deliberate in waking up her pleasure and I was gifted with tiny little whimpers that turned into hot sordid moans of my name.

I wanted to be the one to corrupt every inch of her. And I took joy in it.

She cried out so sweetly as my tongue lapped at her sweet center. Curling around that hard little bundle of nerves before dipping down the crevice until it reached that tightened rosebud. Over and over again, I lapped at her hungrily, dipping my fingers into her and sucking on her until she was lifting her hips off the bed. Rolling them up in the air, her hand placed securely on the back of my head as she forced me to drink from those pure juices.

"Beau," my name became her orgasm as she shuddered and merged, the entire time I drank and sucked and slithered my tongue over her sensitive clit.

She was murmuring nonsense as I tore my pants and shirt off. Her eyelids half opened, her pink lips parted, her breaths ragged from my savagery.

I slid over again, my hands dragging up her body to cup

her breasts. My mouth was hovering against her lips. It wasn't until my cock dragged up her center that she tensed beneath me.

Her eyes flew open, and she fixed them on me.

I caressed her cheek softly and she blinked, staring at me as if I were some sort of apparition.

"You're real."

"I'm real." I frowned and stared down at her for a long time. "Do you remember?"

She shook her head. "Not everything."

I pulled back, stunned. "You don't remember us."

"I remember you from my dreams. You're Beau."

She traced my face with her fingertips. "You're mine."

My heart, beat rapidly, and my body lit up at her words. "Yes, I am yours."

"How did you find me?"

I shook my head, realizing now that I wasn't the one to find her. "I didn't. You called out to me."

She smiled, arching her hips up and making me growl in satisfaction.

"Is it true?"

"What's that, sweets?"

"That you love me."

"I've loved you forever."

"Don't leave me, again. Okay."

"I won't be leaving you ever again."

I slid myself inside of her, and we both gasped against each other's lips as I forced my cock in deep. There was no pain this time, just that sweet sound of pleasure that emanated from us both.

I began to move, thrusting into her lithe body as she tugged on my hair, her nails digging into my skin as I fucked her.

"Beg me, Elora. Tell me what you need."

She was torn between what was happening and what she felt. Her hands ran up my arms, her nails dragging down around my shoulders. Her body tensed, and the muscles at her core clamped around me making me give out a low deep rumble of aching need.

"I need you. Don't stop."

I did as she asked. Fucking her hard and deep, her breasts trembling erotically with every thrust. I bent down and kissed her, a holy prayer said just between us as I took back what had been stolen from me so long ago.

Her cries of pleasure broke the kiss and as her body shuddered from another orgasm I reared back, watching her come undone while she had me trapped inside of her.

"Never leave," she murmured, and I grinned as I took her again. Rutting inside her like the hellhound that once had lain in me. Just an animal in heat for the one that belonged to him.

She came again, arching back, a guttural purr came from her as I held her down, while our hips rolled against one another. She cradled my face and continued to breathe raggedly as she moved against me.

I turned us, lifting her on me as she slid me inside. My eyes never left her as she undulated, swirling those hips on me and bouncing as she fucked herself.

"Use me," I whispered, and she obeyed.

Rocking back on my cock and sliding herself up and down on it. That sweet pussy inhaling me and sucking me up into delirium.

"Fuck me, Elora."

She whimpered as she leaned down over me, nipping at my lip.

"You make me feel so good," she whimpered.

I grabbed her ass, holding her hips still, her body pressed against me as I lifted my hips into her. Thrusting my cock in quick deliberate ruts. She cried out, holding on as another orgasm tore through her.

This was the joys of what being alive meant. This yearning and need being finally fulfilled. She laughed as she slid off me. And with a hint in her eye, she scooted off my lap and down between my legs. I watched her as she took my swollen well-used cock in her hand. She gave me a knowing smile before wrapping that pretty little mouth around it. My mouth opened and I rumbled as I lifted my hips, sliding my dick onto her tongue. She felt fucking glorious as she sucked at me. That innocent mouth doing the most wicked of things.

"I'm gonna cum."

She hummed around me, and I lost all my senses. I lay there as she squeezed out every drop. Drinking from me and coating herself in my cream. When she was done, she lay alongside me. Rubbing at my chest.

"You are real."

"I am."

She stayed quiet for a little bit and then broke the silence. "If you're real then they're real. Aren't they?"

I knew what she meant. I now realized she'd been dreaming of her memories for all these years.

"They could be. If you allow them to be."

She hugged me tight. "I could feel you so deeply in my dreams."

"That's because I was there, Elora. I've been there with you all along."

"Don't ever leave again, okay." She repeated and, in some way, I sensed her fear.

Now that you had what you longed for, it was only human to fear it being taken away.

I smiled and ran my hand through her hair and down her back, soothingly.

"I don't plan on it."

She was slowly falling back asleep. "I don't think I can live without you."

I looked up at the ceiling knowing I couldn't either. And as she drifted off to sleep, she murmured the phrase I'd been waiting to hear.

"I love you so much."

And with that, I was once again condemned to roam the earth with my love by my side, while I made sure to keep her safe from the demons that lay claim on her.

Karma

EPILOGUE TWO

Reflections of theFallen

He appeared in a cloud of smoke and flames and the burning scent of brimstone filled the air. His wings half torn off; his massive, muscled body bruised. He reached out his hand to me and I tried grabbing his, but he was too far away. Our fingertips touched, heat coiling through me just as his words reached me.

"Help me, witch."

I gasped for air, jerking up in bed, kicking at my sheets as they'd twisted around my ankles. What in the world was that, and who was he?

I've been having night terrors for a few years now. I hadn't had them since I was little. But these were far too vivid. That demon felt all too real, yet it was as if I knew him.

I hadn't practiced magic in a long time. Only blessings and assisting Elora with her mother's store. For the last few years, I'd felt life pass me by as if in a thick fog. I felt like I had lost a lifetime. Like something was missing.

The nightmares had only gotten worse since that man had come into Elora's life talking about lost memories and lost love. I didn't know what to make of it, but Elora was beyond happy, and he was adamant in showing his love. So who was I to ruin that.

My feet felt heavy as I dragged myself to the bathroom, flicking on the light as I approached the mirror. I looked tired, as if I'd waged a war tonight. I tugged at my eyes, lightly pulling on the dark circles that had formed.

I was so concentrated on washing my face and hands, that when the lights in the bathroom went out, I merely shrugged it off. That had also been happening much more frequently.

I turned, searching blindly for the light switch. When I flipped it on, nothing happened. I drew a deep frustrated exhale, and as I turned to walk out, the menacing appearance of a dark shadow figure stopped me in my tracks. I gasped as the apparition took a step closer, and I blinked a few times willing my eyes to clear up.

"Wake up, Karma. Come on, wake up."

As the apparition came closer, I realized this was not one of my nightmares. I was awake, and I was no longer alone. The knowledge of that was sudden and frightening. There he was. Reaching out for me, his eyes torn in anguish.

I screamed, the image startling as I stumbled to the floor. I scrambled back along the cold tile, while he continued his pursuit. Every slide back, he would take a step forward until I was trapped against the tile wall.

He fell to one knee before me, his features half hidden. If I wasn't so scared of him, I'd say he was beautiful in his magnitude.

With shaking fingers, I reached out along the wall, fumbling in the dark for the switch. He was so close; I could smell the smoke and brimstone coming off him.

"Help me, witch."

Those same words were whispered in my face, just as my fingers found the switch. Light engulfed the room and the apparition disappeared. I took a deep breath. Pulling my legs under me, holding them tightly as I curled up into a fetal position.

This couldn't be happening.

This isn't happening.

And then suddenly, I heard that voice again. This time it was whispered in my ear, the hot breath of that demon making the strands of my hair move.

"Help me, Karma."

I screamed again, only this time I couldn't stop.

About the Author

Thank you for reading!

If you enjoyed Beau & Elora's story, please don't hesitate to leave your reviews. I do love to hear what sinful thoughts my readers throw my way!

Stay tuned for more in the Empire of the Fallen series with a fallen angel and his witch. Kimaris and Karma are next in **Broken Requiem**!

Follow me for more of my sexy alphas and step into my MC World: including the Hell-bound Lovers MC, the Royal Bastards MC & the Death Row Shooters MC.
http://bit.ly/AuthorCrimsonSyn

If you want more if my trigger-filled romances, check out Devious Heart and Insidious Love on Amazon-Free on Kindle!

Meet the Royal Bastards MC: www. royalbastardsmc.com

For RBMC & Hellbound Lovers Swag check out my Synful Swag Store here:

https://www.teepublic.com/user/synfulswag

To get the inside scoop, teasers, new release reviews and dirty details of my upcoming series sign up for the mailing list. You'll receive a free copy of Sweet Temptress when you sign up!

http://eepurl.com/cFxRu9

facebook.com/crimsonsynromance

twitter.com/CrimsonSyn82

Also by Crimson Syn

HELLBOUND LOVERS MC

WOLF (Hellbound Lovers MC #1)

GRAYSON (Hellbound Lovers MC #2)

RIGGS (Hellbound Lovers MC #3)

CAIN (Hellbound Lovers MC #4)

SETH (Hellbound Lovers MC #5)

GUNNER (Hellbound Lovers MC #6)

DIESEL (Hellbound Lovers MC #7)

KNOX (Hellbound Lovers MC #8)

HELLBOUND LOVERS MC SIDE STORY

Dirty Cupid: A Reverse Harem HLMC

HELLBOUND LOVERS MC PREQUELS

RYDER

BEAR

HAIL

SINFUL HOLIDAY NOVELLAS

A Wicked Treat

Dreams by the Fire

Sinful Valentine Wishes

Christmas Angel

STANDALONE NOVELS

Coveted Desire

Empire of the Fallen PNR/Shifter Romance Series

Bane & Bound: Twisted Legends Collections

DEVIOUS HEART SERIES

Devious Heart

Insidious Love

Bless Me, Father

EDGE BDSM SERIES

EDGE

WIDOW

RAVENHEAD CORPORATION SERIES

Dirty Obsession

Beautiful Betrayal

Filthy Seduction

DEATH ROW SHOOTERS MC

REAPER (Death Row Shooters MC #1)

POET (Death Row Shooters MC #2)

VINDICATOR (Death Row Shooters MC #3)

ROYAL BASTARDS MC

New Orleans National Chapter

Inked In Vengeance

Printed in Great Britain
by Amazon